Woman with Horns and Other Stories
US Edition

CECILIA MANGUERRA BRAINARD

Published by PALH

(Philippine American Literary House)
P.O. Box 5099
Santa Monica, CA 90409, USA
PALHBOOKS.com; palh@aol.com

ISBN: 978-1-953716-03-3 (Paperback edition)
ISBN: 978-1-953716-04-0 (Ebook edition)

Woman with Horns and Other Stories was first published by
New Day Publishers in 1987, Copyright © 1987 Cecilia
Manguerra Brainard. All rights belong to the author.

INTRODUCTION

The reception of Cecilia Manguerra Brainard's first short story collection, *Woman with Horns and Other Stories*, published in 1987, has been extraordinary. Her mythical place "Ubec" (Cebu backwards) was embraced by Cebuanos and "Ubec" and has become part of their lexicon. Teachers use stories from this collection and YouTube has student films of the story "Woman with Horns" in particular. There is even a Wikipedia write-up about "Woman with Horns."

The book collects a dozen stories that draw from historical and contemporary sources. Many of these stories explore the clash of Philippine culture with foreign influences that reached the archipelago during different historical periods.

Katipunan praised the books as follows, "Beautifully written in the minimalist style yet never lacking color and clarity, Brainard's stories reach out from the deep centuries of folklore, superstition, religion, customs, geography and history to bring them life into the present. But more than life itself, this book mirrors the unique ways in which the Filipina woman searches for meaning. The locale and period of each story expand rather than limit the characters' choices."

The US edition of *Woman with Horns and Other Stories* presents this beloved book to a new audience and ones who may have read Brainard's subsequent works after *Woman with Horns and Other Stories*, including her novels, *When the Rainbow Goddess Wept, Magdalena*, and *The Newspaper Widow*.

CONTENTS

ACKNOWLEDGMENTS

First published by New Day Publishers in the Philippines in 1987, *Woman with Horns and Other Stories*, is published in the US by PALH (Philippine American Literary House) in 2020. All rights belong to the author Cecilia Manguerra Brainard.

"Alba" appeared in *Studia Mystica* (Summer, 1986), and *Making Waves*, Beacon Press 1989.

"The Balete Tree" was published in *St. Andrews Review*, No. 29 (1986); it was the winner of the 1985 Fortner Prize.

"The Black Man in the Forest" appeared in *Amerasia Journal,* Vol. 12, No. 1 (1985-86). and *Filipino Women in America: 1860-1986.*

"The Blue-Green Chiffon Dress" was published in *Focus Philippines* (September 1984), *Home to Stay* (The Greenfield Review Press 1990), and *The Perimeter of Light* (New Rivers Press 1992).

"Miracle at Santo Niño Church was published in *Focus Philippines* (September 1984).

"Trinidad's Brooch" was published in *Songs of Ourselves: Writings by Filipino Women in English* (Anvil 1994).

"Waiting for Papa's Return" appeared in *Making Waves* (Asian Women United 1989). *Home to Stay* (The Greenfield Review Press 1990). Writers' Program Quarterly of UCLA Extension (Fall 1990), and *Asian American Literature* (Glencoe McGraw-Hill 2001).

"Woman with Horns" was published in *Focus Philippines* (July 1984).

WOMAN WITH HORNS

DR. GERALD MCALLISTER listened to the rattle of doors being locked and footsteps clattering on the marble floors. The doctors and nurses were hurrying home. It was almost noon and the people of Ubec always lunched in their dining rooms with high ceilings, where their servants served soup, fish, meat, rice, and rich syrupy flan for dessert. After, they retired to their spacious airy rooms for their midday siesta. At three, they resumed work or their studies.

His assistant, Dr. Jaime Laurel, had explained that the practice was due to the tropical heat and high humidity. Even the dogs, he had pointed out, retreated under houses and shade trees.

Gerald could not understand this local custom. An hour for lunch should be more than enough. He barely had that when he was a practicing physician in New York.

He reread his report about the cholera epidemic in the southern town of Carcar. Thanks to his vaccination program, the epidemic was now under control. The success was another feather in his cap, one of many he had accumulated during his stay in the Philippine Islands. No doubt Governor General Taft or perhaps even President McKinley would send him a letter of commendation. Politicians were like that; they appreciated information justifying America's hold on the

1

archipelago.

He glanced at the calendar on his ornate desk. It was March 16, 1903, a year and a half since he arrived at the Port of Ubec aboard the huge steamship from San Francisco. Three years since Blanche died.

His head hurt and he removed his glasses to stroke his forehead. When the headache passed, he straightened out the papers on his desk and left the office. The quiet of his wing of the Ubec General Hospital annoyed him as he walked past locked doors, potted palms, and sand-filled spittoons.

In front of Dr. Laurel's office, he saw a woman trying to open the door. She looked distraught and wrung her hands. She was a native Ubecan — Gerald had seen her at the Mayor's functions —a comely woman with bronze skin and long hair so dark it glinted blue. She wore a long blue satin skirt. An embroidered *panuelo* over her *camisa* was pinned to her bosom with a magnificent brooch of gold and pearls.

"It is lunchtime," he said in English. His Spanish was bad and his Ubecan dialect far worse.

Dark fiery eyes flashed at him.

"*Comer*," he said, gesturing with his right hand to his mouth.

"I know it's lunchtime. It wasn't, fifteen minutes ago." She tried the door once more and slapped her skirt in frustration. Tears started welling in her eyes. "My husband died over a year ago."

"I'm sorry."

"I'm not. He was in pain for years. Consumption. I have been coughing and last night, I dreamt of a funeral. I became afraid. I have a daughter, you see."

"Dr. Laurel will return at three."

"You are a doctor. American doctors are supposed to be the best. Can you help me?"

"I don't see patients."

"Ahh," she said, curved eyebrows rising. She picked up her fan with a gold chain pinned to her skirt. "Ahh, a doctor who doesn't see patients." She fanned herself slowly.

Her words irritated him and he brusquely said, "Come back in a few hours; Dr. Laurel will be back then." She stood there with eyes still moist, her neck tilted gracefully to one side and her hand languorously moving the fan back and forth.

"It was nothing," Jaime said. "I listened to her chest and back. There are no lesions, no T.B. I told her to return in a month. I think she is spectacular; she can come back for checkups forever." With mischief in his eyes, he added, "Agustina Macaraig has skin like velvet; if she were not my patient — "

"Jaime, your oath. You and your women. Doesn't your wife mind?" Gerald said.

"Eh, she's the mother of my children, is she not?" Shrugging his shoulders, he fixed the Panama hat on his head.

It was late Friday afternoon and they were promenading in the park, trying to catch the cool sea breeze. The park was in front of an old Spanish fort. There was a playground in the middle and benches were scattered under the surrounding acacia and mango trees. Children led by their *yayas* crowded the playground. Men and women walked or huddled together to talk about the day's events.

As he walked by the playground, Gerald was surprised to see Agustina pushing a girl of around five on the swing. When the child pleaded to do the pushing, Agustina got on the swing. He watched her kick her legs out and throw her head back, her blue-black hair flying about. She was laughing, oblivious to the scandal she was causing.

"The people don't approve of her," Gerald commented when he noticed women gossiping behind their fans, their eyes riveted on Agustina.

"There is a saying in Ubec, 'A mango tree cannot bear avocados,'" Jaime continued.

Gerald shrugged his shoulders.

"Look at her. Is she not delectable?" Jaime said. "People say she is wicked, like her mother. She has a very

3

mysterious background."

They sat on a bench next to a blooming hibiscus bush where they could see her. The child pushed her hard and Agustina's infectious laughter rose above other sounds.

"I can see why the people would despise a widow who carries on the way she does," Gerald said.

"But, friend, you don't understand. We love her. She is one of us. It's just that Ubecans love to gossip, even when she patiently nursed her husband. They said she had lovers, but for five years, she took care of him. The people of Ubec like to talk. Over their meals, they talk; after eating, they talk; outside church after worshipping God, they talk; during afternoon walks, they talk. Just like we're talking, no?"

"I did not come here to gossip. I was perfectly content planning my bubonic plague campaign when you —"

"Friend, you don't know how to enjoy life. Look at that sun turning red, getting ready to set spectacularly. It is a wonderful afternoon, you walk with a friend, you talk about beautiful women, about life. Now, let me finish my story. People say her mother — a simple laundry woman —jumped over the seminary walls and behind those hallowed walls, under the arbol de fuego trees, she bedded with one of Christ's chosen."

"Ridiculous!"

"Ridiculous, nothing," Jaime replied as he pulled out a cigar from his pocket and offered it to Gerald. "Tabacalera, almost as good as Havanas."

Gerald shook his head. "Thank you, but I don't smoke."

"You don't smoke; you don't have women; you are a shell. Bringing you here was a chore. Are all American doctors like yourself? If they are, I wouldn't be caught dead in your rich and great country. You look like a god from Olympus — tall, blonde with gray eyes. You're not forty, yet you act like an old man."

"Jaime, skip your lecture and get on with your story." Gerald watched Agustina loll her head back. She was biting her lower lip, afraid of how high she was.

"If you were not my boss, I would shake you to your senses. Anyway, the story goes that Agustina was born with horns."

"Horns?"

"Like *toro*, yes." Jaime put his finger to his forehead. "At noon, her mother went to the enchanted river to do her wash. The spirits roam at that time, do you know that?"

Gerald shook his head at this nonsense. "I swim almost daily at your so-called enchanted river and I have seen nothing but fish and an occasional water buffalo. Filthy animals."

"Well, maybe there are or aren't spirits, no? Who are we to say there are none? The people say that her mother had — ah, how do you say —an encounter with an *encantado*, a river spirit. And Agustina is the product of that brief encounter."

Gerald watched her jump off the swing, her skirt swirling up, her shapely legs flashing before his eyes.

"She doesn't look much like a river spirit's daughter, Jaime," Gerald said with a snort.

"Beware, you can never be sure."

She took the girl's hand and they ran to a group of women. Agustina carried on an animated conversation then waved goodbye. Before she turned to leave the park, she looked briefly at Gerald. He caught her gaze but she quickly lowered her eyes and walked away as if she had not seen him.

On the way to the Mayor's house, Gerald thought that attending social functions was part of his job. He was not only Ubec's Public Health Director, he was also an ambassador-of-sorts for the United States. The truth was, he didn't really mind social affairs at all. They kept him occupied. When he was busy, he didn't have time to think about the past, to feel that shakiness, that pain that had possessed him after Blanche died.

During the day he was fine; he worked, lunched, swam, went on promenades, had rich frothy chocolate with the men. Later he dined, sipped after-dinner brandies and liqueurs, and chatted until way past midnight. It was when the servants locked the doors and the house was still, when the only sound was the lonely chatter of the night watchman, that he would feel his composure slip away. His heart would palpitate and an uneasiness would overcome him. He would try to cram his mind with thoughts — health education campaigns, sanitation programs, quarantine reports — but the disquiet would stay with him.

The Mayor of Ubec, a small round man, greeted Gerald warmly. He introduced him as the great American doctor who was wiping out cholera, smallpox, and bubonic plague from Ubec. The people knew him of course and they shook his hand heartily. They congratulated him on his recent success in Carcar and inquired about his current bubonic plague campaign. Rats, Gerald explained, transmit the disease; therefore getting rid of the pest by traps and arsenic poisoning would eliminate the problem.

When the food was served on the long dining table with tall silver candelabras, the Mayor teased Dr. McAllister for his squeamishness at the roasted pig. The women giggled demurely, covering their mouths with their hand-painted fans or lace handkerchiefs, while the men laughed boisterously. The Mayor's mother, a fat old woman with a mustache, tore off the pig's ear and pressed it in Gerald's hand. "Taste it, my American son," she said. Laughing and clapping, the people urged him to take a bite until he finally did.

When he later went to the verandah to drink his rice wine, he saw Agustina standing there, gazing at the stars. She looked different, not the frightened woman at the hospital, not the carefree girl at the park, but a proper Ubecan widow in black, with her hair done in a severe bun. Curiously, the starkness enhanced her grace and beauty, calling attention to the curves of her body.

"You did not like the *lechon*?" she asked softly, with an amused twinkle in her eyes.

"I beg your pardon? Oh, the pig —?" He shook his head, embarrassed that she had witnessed that charade. They were alone and he hoped that someone would join them.

"What do Americans eat, Dr. McAllister?" She was studying him, eyes half-closed with a one-sided smile that was becoming.

Gerald pushed his hair from his forehead. "Pies -- cherry pies, boysenberry pies -- I miss them all. Frankly, I have — "

She drew closer to him and he caught a warm, musky scent coming from her body.

"—I have lost ten pounds since I've been here."

"In kilos, how many?"

"Around four and a half."

"Santa Clara! You must get rid of your cook. She must be an incompetent, starving you like that. It is a shame to the people of Ubec!"

Gerald watched her, aware of his growing infatuation.

"I like you," she said suddenly. "You and I have a kinship. Come to my house and my daughter and I will feed you." Pausing, she reached up to stroke his face with her fan. His cheeks burned. "Nothing exotic," she continued, "just something good." Her eyes flashed as she smiled. "You know where I live?"

He hesitated then shook his head. His knees were shaking.

"The house at the mouth of the river. I see you swimming during siesta time. I like to swim at night, when the moon is full." She looked at him, closed her eyes languidly and walked away.

After dinner, Gerald hurried home and paced his bedroom floor. He should have been flattered by Agustina's advances, but instead he was angry and confused. She was enchanting and desirable and he was upset that he should find her so.

Once he had been unfaithful when Blanche was bedridden. The surgical nurse who laughed a lot had been willing, and he had wanted even for just a few hours to forget, to be happy. Blanche had known, just by looking at him. "Oh, Tiger, how could you? How could you?" After her death, he had not given this side of himself a thought. Yet now, he found himself recalling that indescribable musky-woman scent emanating from Agustina.

There was something else. It bothered him deeply that Agustina, widowed for only a little over a year, would laugh, be happy, even flirt outrageously with him. Why was she not consumed with grief? Why did she not sit at home crocheting white doilies? Why did she not light candles in the crumbling musty churches, the way proper Ubecan widows did? He was outraged at her behavior. He condemned her for the life that oozed out of her, when he needed every ounce of his strength just to stay sane.

He strode to his desk and stared at the album with photographs, which he had not looked at in years. The wedding picture showed a vibrant smiling young woman with a ring of tiny white flowers around her blonde curly hair. His face was unlined then, and his mustache seemed an affectation. Anxious eyes peered through round eyeglasses, as if he knew even then that the future would give him anguish.

He studied the other pictures — serious daguerreotypes — that unleased a flood of emotions. He found himself weeping at some, smiling at others. He remembered Blanche's soft voice: "Oh, Tiger, I adore you so." Blanche in bed, waiting for him. And later, Blanche in bed, pale, thin, with limp hair. She had been eaten bit by bit by consumption; she had been consumed, until only a skeleton that coughed incessantly and spat blood remained. Gerald did not believe in God, but he had prayed for her death, just so it would end. When she died, he was surprised to feel another kind of grief, more acute, more searing.

After her funeral, his mind would go on and on about how useless he was — a doctor whose wife died of consumption was a failure. And always the soft voice: Oh, Tiger, how could you?

Returning from work each night, he had found himself waiting for her voice: How was your day, Tiger? He saw slight women with curly blonde hair and he had followed them. He plunged into a depression — not eating, unable to work, to think clearly, to talk coherently. He stayed shut up in his room with wine-colored drapes. At times he thought he was losing his mind. When he pointed a gun to his forehead, a part of him panicked and said: NO. That part had taken over and started running his life again. Eat, so you will gain weight; exercise, so your body will be healthy; work, so your mind will not dwell on the agony.

It was this part that had led him to the Islands, far away from slight women with curly blonde hair. It was this same part that now said: Blanche is dead, you are alive; you have the right to laugh and be happy just as Agustina laughs and is happy.

Gerald struggled with himself but would not allow himself to surrender his mourning. He decided not to see Agustina; he would not allow her to corrupt him.

Governor General William H. Taft's handwritten letter from Manila arrived that morning and Gerald reread it several times, trying to absorb the congratulatory words. He felt nothing. He would not have cared if the letter had never come. He realized that he didn't really care, nowadays. Work was predictable; there was little risk. He applied himself and the laurels came. But the successes, the commendations did not fill his emptiness. He picked up the conch shell that he used as a paper weight and tapped it, listening to the hollow ring that echoed in his office.

Gerald went to Jaime's office to show him the letter. Jaime appeared cross; he sat erect and immobile as he listened quietly.

"Well?" Gerald asked after reading the letter aloud.

"Well, what?"

"The letter — it's a fine letter, don't you think?" He hoped for an enthusiastic reply that would rub some life into him.

"The Mayor's mother is dead," Jaime said. "She choked on some food."

"Too bad. Well, at least it wasn't typhoid or anything contagious," he said.

Jaime's black eyes snapped at him. "You bastard!" he said. "All you think about is work. You have no soul."

Gerald could not work the rest of the morning. He felt a growing restlessness, a vague uneasiness that he could not pinpoint. No soul. Had he indeed lost his soul? Was that why he could not feel and why he didn't care about anything? In trying to bring order to his life, in restructuring it after Blanche died, had he lost a vital part of himself — his soul?

Funerals, Gerald thought as he walked to the Mayor's house, were dreary, maudlin affairs, where people wore long faces and tried to sound sincere as they dug up some memory of the deceased.

He braced himself when he saw mourners in black and the huge black bow on the Mayor's front door. Inside, he was surprised to see the number of people crowding the place. Some wept; others laughed and related stories about the old woman. A rather festive air filled the place.

The Mayor hugged Gerald, saying, "What a tragedy, what a tragedy! She was eating pickled pig snout when suddenly she choked. It was over before any of us could do anything. She loved you like a son and worried that you were too thin."

"I'm sorry," mumbled Gerald.

The Mayor brought him to the casket in the living room. "Mama chose her own funeral picture," the Mayor said as he pointed at the huge picture of a slim young girl, propped up next to the coffin. "She was a vain woman. The picture was taken almost half a century ago."

The Mayor continued, "Her mind was not clear. She wanted to be buried in her wedding gown but it was far too small. I had to hire three seamstresses to work all night. They ripped and stitched, adding panels of cloth to the dress. It was still too small. Finally we decided to clothe her in another dress and to lay her wedding gown on top, pinning it here and there to keep it in place. Family deaths can be trying," he said.

The old Spanish friar said a Latin Mass and spoke lengthily about her goodness and kindness. "She had a rich and long life," he concluded. Near the hearse, an old man riding a horse stopped them. He was dressed in a revolutionary uniform with medals hanging on his chest, and a gun in his right hand which he fired once. Gasping, the mourners stopped still. The old man ordered the men to open the casket. He got off his horse, bent over the casket and planted a kiss on the corpse's lips. Then, he got back on his horse and galloped off.

It took a while for the mourners to compose themselves and continue to the cemetery. A pair of scissor was placed under the satin pillow; family members kissed the body; the priest blessed the coffin and she was finally buried.

Everybody returned to the Mayor's house for a huge banquet. Jaime tried to explain the revelry by saying that a person was feted on his birth, his marriage, and his death. "It's the end of a good life, my friend," he said.

Agustina, who was there, walked up to Gerald. "It was a beautiful funeral," she said.

"I've never attended one like it," he replied and laughed. "I guess it was."

They were near a window and she looked out. "Ahh, the moon is full."

From his room, Gerald watched the large moon rise, shining on the star apple and jackfruit trees in his backyard. It was a warm night, even with all the windows open. He waited for even the slightest breeze to stir the silvery leaves, but there was no wind and a restlessness grew in him.

At last he decided to go to the river. Silence and oppressive heat dominated Ubec as he walked the cobblestones. He reached the path leading to the river and the sea. The moon was so bright that the air seemed to vibrate as he followed the trail that widened, then narrowed, then widened again, until he reached the riverbank.

After leaving his things under a coconut tree, he walked to the water and saw how clear it was. Little gray fish darted between colorful rocks. In the distance the river and sea shimmered brilliantly.

The water felt cool and silky. Gerald swam back and forth, marveling at the brazenness of the fish that brushed against him, some even nibbling his toes. He spotted a bright green rock and wondered about it. Diving to the river bottom, he fetched it. When he surfaced, he saw her standing next to his things. He was not surprised; he knew she would be there.

Moonlight bathed her, making her glow. A green and red *tapis* was wrapped around her, exposing golden shoulders and neck, showing mounds of flesh.

Gerald felt life stirring in him and, holding his breath, he waded to the shore. She walked toward him. The water splashed and the small gray fish skittered away when she slipped into the water. He watched the river creep higher and higher as her *tapis* floated gracefully around her, until they fell into each other's arms.

THE BLACK MAN IN THE FOREST

Philippines, 1901

BY MID-DAY, the old general and his men stumbled into that part of the forest where they felt they could stop and make camp. The stronger men immediately searched for food; some dug for roots, others set traps for lizards and sparrows. The skin-and-bones ones collapsed in heaps under the bushes.

General Gregorio studied his men then did something he instructed them never to do -- he left the scraggly group of soldiers and walked to the river. He drank some water and sat on a boulder to contemplate his situation. He had seven men, three guns, ten bullets, and eight rusty machetes. They had no food nor medicines. Even before this point of desperation, they had relied on saliva, herbs, and faith to heal their wounded who eventually died and were buried in unmarked graves as his army was driven back into the mountains by the Americans.

He stared at his gun with two bullets and the machete hanging from his belt, and he snorted at his fate. Their only hope was to find General Macario and his regiment. Otherwise they would all be killed by the snotty-nosed Americans — young enough to be his grandchildren — with their blue uniforms and Krag rifles.

General Gregorio was thinking this when a shot split

through his reverie, knocking him over. He felt a sharp sting on his left thigh, then warm fluid oozing down his leg to the river bank. When he fell, his hand had been on the gun and he lay there not breathing, willing his heart to be still. The general heard the crunching of twigs, the rustling of bushes, and heavy footsteps. He felt a foot poke him in the back. When he heard the metallic sound of a rifle being cocked, General Gregorio swiftly rolled over and aimed his gun. He fired a bullet that entered the forehead of a black soldier. With a frozen look the black man cried, "Sara," then crumpled.

Although his left leg felt like burning coal, the general got up and fired the remaining bullet into the man's chest. Then he kicked the soldier's rifle away. Certain that the man was dead, the general went to the river and ripped his pants to tend his wound. He washed it and squeezed the flesh around the bullet hole to force tainted blood out. It was a clean wound; the bullet had gone straight through, and the general was relieved. He had seen too many wounds fester. He had watched men lose parts of themselves, first a hand, then an arm, until their brains went into delirium from the poison travelling through their arteries and finally they died.

All his men, even the frailest with death looking over his shoulders, rushed to the river. They were shouting, waving their guns and machetes. One of them thrust his knife into the black man's heart. The small dark one among them who had healing hands went to General Gregorio and inspected his leg. He tied a piece of cloth around the general's thigh to slow the bleeding and said they would have to use the juice of guava shoots to hasten cure. "The dampness of the forest," he said looking around, "is not good for this."

The general realized that his legs were wobbly and that his hands were shaking fiercely. Embarrassed at his weakness, he shooed away the little man who then joined the others around the corpse.

"If not for his uniform, I'd swear he was an *agta* or some other enchanted being," said the soldier whom they called Liver-eater. He was a big man from the north who liked to eat his enemies' livers for courage.

"He is big but he's not enchanted," another replied. "I have seen black men among the enemy."

Liver-eater spat on the ground next to the body. "I have seen only the ones like albinos with hair the color of corn kernels. Some have cat-eyes; scared the shit out of me. But the albino-types — their liver is filled with bile and tastes bitter.

The small dark one knelt down and put his hand against the soldier's hand. "Look, he's darker than me. He must have been under the sun for a long time. And his arm is twice as long as mine. He must have eaten well." The small man pinched the soldier's arm. "Damn, the man's got flesh! This man ate meat and all the rice he wanted. None of that fish and corn meal I grew up on. He had thick goat's milk, butter so rich it made you dizzy, and sticky wild honey."

The talk of food made them sigh, even General Gregorio. Their mouths watered at the thought of real food; their spirits longed for companionable meals with charming women and happy children. Their minds began fixing on memories: Christmas dinners with families where they gorged on roasted pig and pickled papaya; picnics where they feasted on enormous Lapu-Lapu fish stuffed with tomatoes and herbs; May fiestas with hams, potatoes, and sweet gelatinous desserts. They had subsisted on roots and lizards, listened to children wailing, smelled the stench of blood for so long.

"Well, now," General Gregorio said to snap them out of their dreams, "there might be more Americans around." He ordered some men to patrol the area and told the rest to continue with their business. "I'll handle the dead man and I'll distribute his belongings tonight," spoke the general.

All but Liver-eater left. With feet planted apart, he stared evenly at the general, stubbornly refusing to budge. "We'll see," the general said in a loud voice, standing erect on his weak legs until Liver-eater walked away.

General Gregorio had been a soldier for enough time for a chico tree to grow from a seed to maturity. He had personally killed seventeen Spaniards, Americans, and even

Filipinos. Once, he had hanged a handsome, big-bosomed woman who had betrayed them. He had done many things to survive, to make his beliefs reality, but he did not consider himself a barbaric man, and eating human flesh was abhorrent to him.

He began to feel dizzy so he sat on the ground and put his head between his legs. When his head cleared, he checked his leg once more, tightening the cloth, muttering *merde* because of the excruciating pain that radiated to the tip of his hair. He was an old soldier and he had been hurt before. He had two giant scars: a saber-mark on his right arm and a machete-gash on his back; but he had never been hit by a bullet until now. An anger welled in him. If the wound rots, he could lose his leg, he could die — the general glared at the dead man wishing there was still life in him so he could snuff it out again. But the black soldier was immobile like a beached whale, with flies buzzing over him, some sucking his blood. General Gregorio noticed that the man's eyes were open. The dead man still had the frozen expression of terror on his face. General Gregorio felt a sense of elation, of vengeance.

But soon his elation gave way to fear because the soldier seemed to be staring across the river. Afraid of an enemy attack, the general glanced that way but saw only huge rocks, thick vegetation, and monkeys swinging in the branches. Shafts of sunlight streamed into the forest. In the distance parrots screeched.

Calming himself, the general turned to the black man once more. He observed the neat little hole on his forehead and the blood crusting on his springy black hair. The dead man's mouth was slightly open, still saying the "a" of Sara. The general flicked the flies of the man's face, wondering who Sara was. Years ago, when the Spaniard had swung his saber at his face and his right hand had flown up to catch the sword, General Gregorio had shouted "Mama." When the traitorous Filipino threw the machete at his back, he had called out "Marta." Sara must be his wife or lover, thought the general. Instantly he had the mental image of a young woman with skin the color of narra wood, humming as she scattered sliced onions over a thick slab of meat.

Shivering at his vision, the general proceeded to gather the man's possessions: a rifle, thirty bullets, a pair of leather boots barely scuffed, a chewed-up bit of beef jerky, a gold pocket watch, a knife, some silver coins, but no pictures, no papers of identity whatsoever. In this forest, on this river bank, this black man was nameless. And yet, the general thought, surely he did have a name. He most certainly had a mother who had carried him in her womb, brought him into the world, and gave him a name. There was a woman Sara whom he remembered even as the bullet pierced his skull — and surely Sara called this man by name. The general became somber at these thoughts and he felt a longing to name his person. He called him John because it seemed that many Americans were named John.

John's eyes made the general uneasy so he closed the eyelids stretching the skin over the troubled eyes. Then the general forced the black man's jaws together. General Gregorio sat back and tried to imagine a hint of peace on that face. But the blood on the forehead and chest troubled him. Ignoring his pain, the general dragged the man near the water and washed the blood from his head and hair. He removed the bloody shirt which he washed in the river, then he cleaned the man's battered chest. As the general rubbed off the sticky blood and poured water over the dark oily skin, a strange feeling crept into the general's heart. He looked at John who was young, strong, and dead. If the black soldier had been a better shot, General Gregorio would have been in his place.

And if he were dead, who would mourn him? His parents had long been dead, his mother dying during childbirth and his father from cholera. Marta, whose memory he nurtured in his soul, was a grandmother to grandchildren who were not his. He had spent so many years being a warrior, a soldier so long that he had forgotten the silky feel of a woman's hair, her gentle laughter; so long that he had forgotten the hush and peace of an old stone church; so long that often he forgot what he was fighting for; so long that he was reduced to fighting for mere survival. He had no real ties, no family, no friends. No one would mourn his death.

This made him sad and this sorrow saturated his being. He waited for the sun and air to dry John's skin and shirt, and before his muscles became rigid, the general put John's shirt back on. It came to General Gregorio then to change John's name to Abraham because it was a more unique name, a name that went better with Sara.

General Gregorio buttoned up Abraham's shirt and covered the buttonhole with his hair. Now Abraham looked better; he appeared like a giant boy sleeping and dreaming troubled dreams.

Liver-eater appeared on the riverside with an insistent face and the general waved him away. When at last Liver-eater begrudgingly left, the general looked at Abraham who was now turning stiff, and he could not bear the idea of Liver-eater getting hold of him. His leg throbbing with pain, the general brought Abraham to the river where the current was strong. He released him and watched the body float downstream until it sank.

Gathering his thoughts, General Gregorio decided to tell his men that the river had risen, taking Abraham away. He would lie to give the black man this bit of dignity. And tomorrow, they would have to start at dawn, before the fog lifted, before the sun's rays slanted into the forest, and they would have to find General Macario and his men, or perish.

TRINIDAD'S BROOCH

UBEC HAD BEEN BLISTERING, cracking from the heat, when overnight it seemed the dry season was over and the typhoons came. It was the seamstress Trinidad's second rainy season in the seaside town and she could not get over the abruptness of change. The rains had always distressed her, even at the orphanage in Manila. Confined to the large marble-floored rooms with the children, nuns, and teachers, Trinidad had listened to the howling winds and lashing rain and had felt alone. Now as she and her assistant Josefa worked, Trinidad's heart pounded with the monotonous drumming of the rain. She was near the window and she peered out through a small opening at the acacia and mango trees in the park. As the winds whipped through, the trees bent and strained. Pausing in the middle of a backstitch with her needle held in mid-air, she wondered if the trees would snap in two.

As if reading her mind Josefa said, "Those trees were planted during the time of Legazpi the Conquistador. Their branches break but they recover and become whole again." Josefa, in her last month of pregnancy, shifted her weight and massaged the small of her back. She was a young, dimple-faced, and talkative woman. "A fisherman drowned last night," she continued. "His mother banged the doors of the rectory. She wailed and pulled her hair because she doesn't even have a body to bury. The old Spanish friar was too deaf to hear the noise. The young one talked to her, but he was so flustered, he forgot to belt his soutane."

Trinidad looked at the flooded streets and stiffened at the image of the foaming sea swallowing up the fisherman. Quiet and serious, she usually paid little attention to Josefa's chatter, but that June afternoon, she listened carefully. However, the pregnant woman turned to other matters: the Mayor was planning a political rally, his mother had dysentery but was better, her cousin Ligaya had grown taller.

Trinidad resumed work but as she made nimble stitches into the fine piña cloth, her bones trembled with the creaking of the tile roof and the groaning of the walls. No matter how tightly she shut the capiz-shell windows, rain seeped in. Water gushed from the sky. The very air smelled damp like rotten mushrooms. It was the rain, she assured herself that afternoon and for the rest of the typhoon season. It was the rain that made her soul flutter on the surface of her skin.

When the rains stopped and the streets dried and the children returned to the park, Trinidad discovered that her unease remained. It was a vague annoyance, like looking at a crooked sleeve or an uneven hemline. She ignored it and prayed but she could not get rid of the gnawing disturbance. Josefa, who had given birth to a baby girl with thick hair that stuck straight up, brought her infant to work. When Josefa nursed her baby one day, Trinidad watched the tiny baby root against her mother's breast until she found the brown nipple dripping with milk. Trinidad felt something inside her strain and pop like the unraveling of a stitch.

That night Trinidad rummaged in her trunk for an antique brooch with a floral design. She ran her forefinger over the jewelry, feeling the smoothness of the pearls and the coldness of the gold setting. Years ago, Mother Asuncion at the orphanage had revealed to her the story about the brooch.

One rainy night, the old nun said, the orphanage bell had rung. Mother Asuncion left the chapel and hurried outside to the turning-cradle where she found Trinidad, an infant whose umbilical cord had not yet dried. The brooch had been pinned to the baby's woven blanket.

At the orphanage, Trinidad had studied the brooch and imagined that her parents were handsome and good. She had told herself that her stay at the Asilo de San Jose was temporary — her parents would return for her. But now, by the light of the flickering lamp, Trinidad stared at the brooch and was overcome with sadness. Her somberness lingered for days. "I don't know — it is nothing," she answered when Josefa asked what was wrong. "Nothing," and she forced herself to embroider the little flowers on a baby girl's gown.

It was her custom to awaken at 4:30 before dawn and walk to the old stone church. By the time the young friar said, "*In nomine Patre*," she was kneeling in the front pew, watching the candles glow before the statues, and smelling melted wax an incense. After Mass, as Mother Asuncion had taught her, Trinidad always stopped by the vigil candle stand to light a candle for thanksgiving — for her life, for her food, for the roof over her head, for everything.

One morning, Trinidad, filled with wordless thoughts and strange feelings, tried to center herself in prayer, but could not. Before Mass ended, she left. She walked past the market vendors, but instead of returning home, went to the seashore. The sun beat down on the desolate sheet of blue water. The bleached sand stretched out empty and forlorn. She sighed a long and deep sigh and continued walking until she found herself near the cemetery. She entered and went from one mausoleum to another, reading the names of the grave markers and counting the number of dead in each family: there were a dozen Santoses, twenty Floreses, and eleven Macaraigs. At the back of the cemetery near the enormous balete tree, she noticed a mound surrounded by abalone shells. It was covered with weeds and a huge rock stood on one end. Sighing, Trinidad knelt down and pulled the vines and grasses. She straightened out the shells. When she finished she wept over the solitary grave.

To force this disquiet from her life, she regimented herself so every moment of her waking hours was accounted for: housework, breakfast, work, lunch, prayers, work, Novena to Our Lady, supper, and prayers. The days and weeks merged one into the other as she possessively protected her spartan schedule. She went through her clothes getting rid of the white dresses with wide collars and ribbons. She sewed clothes of dark browns and blues for herself. She gave away her potted vincas and four o'clock plants, and she stopped adorning her hair with flowers.

Her impatience with Josefa's chatter grew. Trinidad found her and all other Ubecan's tiresome. When they intruded into her organized life, she bristled. She wanted to be left alone; she was not one of them. She found them provincial. They engrossed themselves in other people's affairs, gossiping at all times of the day. They indulged in feasts they could barely afford, for christenings, weddings, funerals. They were superstitious, talking about holy statues walking at night, of spirits and ghosts roaming at dusk, of black giants living in treetops. Although her business prospered, Trinidad regretted having left Manila for Ubec. She cloistered herself in her shop, seeing only those whom she had to. A numbness would occasionally creep inside her, and during these times, she prayed and welcomed even the sensation of irritation at the townspeople.

The rains fell once more and went. Looking around one September day, she realized that the typhoon season had come and gone, and she had felt nothing — no dread, no melancholy, nor annoyance. Even staring at her brooch did not elicit tears. She shivered, thinking she merely was — a woman sitting by the windowsill, sewing still another chemise, crocheting still another lace curtain, embroidering still another chicken into a girl's dress. She sighed — she was dead. She was just as lifeless as the Mayor's mother who had died earlier that day. Trinidad went to her altar to say the litany. During her prayers, the Mayor burst into her dress shop. "You must help," he pleaded. The small round man was very agitated. "Mama, may she rest in peace, wanted to be buried in her wedding gown. But years of content have made her too large for the dress."

Trinidad hastily called Josefa and her cousin Ligaya to help fix the dead woman's gown. They ripped and stitched, attaching panels to the sides, but the woman was far too big, and the dress too small. When the cock crowed and dawn's light filtered into the Mayor's house, they gave up and sewed a loose white shift for the corpse. After clothing the dead woman, they placed the wedding dress on top, pinning it here and there to keep it in place. Josefa arranged the flowers on the casket to mask this deception. Trinidad sewed a large black bow for the Mayor's front door, and another for a huge picture of a young girl. The Mayor explained that this was his mother's funeral picture. "She was vain and her mind had grown unclear. She chose a picture taken when she was fifteen." They propped up the picture beside the coffin in the living room.

They finished in the morning when the mourners in dark clothing were lining outside the Mayor's house to pay their respects to the dead woman. The three women, weary from working overnight left their homes. It was Josefa who, one block away, began chuckling. Ligaya shook her head, covered her mouth with her hand, and laughed softly. Trinidad felt her lips stretch and open as laughter escaped. They stood by the roadside, clutching their sides, laughing for a long time.

She found a spark that glowed in her core and she nurtured it, fanning it as one blows at the embers in the hearth.

23

Shortly after the funeral, Trinidad bought a dozen clay pots in which she planted dahlias, violets, and orchids. She took down her homespun curtains, replacing them with delicate airy lace. While Josefa chatted, she listened, clucked her tongue, and raised her eyebrows at the current gossip. She observed with fascination the little girl who made endless games out of empty spools and polished coconut shells.

One summer afternoon, Trinidad watched Josefa playing with her daughter. The child chortled heartily as her mother tickled her ribs. As Trinidad stared, knowledge rose from the pit of her stomach, filling every part of her body. She would never see her parents, and she would never feel the touch of their hands. Turning away, she looked outside at the sun sinking slowly. Streams of red-orange sunlight sifted through the full sprawling branches of the mango and acacia trees in the park. Before Josefa and the child left, Trinidad went to her trunk to find the gold and pearl brooch. She handed this to Josefa. "It's for the little girl," she said. "Keep it and give it to her when she is old enough. Let her know it came from me."

When the mother and child were gone, Trinidad closed her shop and went to the seashore. It was a late afternoon and the dying sunlight made the sea shimmer like multicolored satin laced with the fine foamy waves. Trinidad paused — she had been an abandoned infant, she thought. She had been an orphan at the Asilo de San Jose; she was now a seamstress in Ubec. And tomorrow — ? Trinidad stared at the hermit crabs skittering about on the sand. Tomorrow, in the morning, Josefa and the child would knock on her shop door, and they would have to finish a wedding gown. She had a pongee skirt to shirr. There were San Francisco cuttings to plant. She sighed and wrapped her arms around herself. Far away the laughter of the fisherman's children tinkled. She closed her eyes and took in the sea breeze. The air was clean, pure. For the moment, this was enough.

THE MAGIC SPRING

GATHERING HER SKIRT around her, the girl hurried down the trail through the bamboo groves marking the entrance to the forest. She glanced around, briefly fearing that the thief of the golden chalice could be nearby. The caw-caw of a bird made her shiver. It was Good Friday and almost dark. A red moon hung in the sky. The spirits were roaming.

The path became narrower while the forest around her thickened. Strange vines falling from gnarled trees brushed her face and body. There was a mixture of animal and plant smells that made her head throb. Now and then she would whisper: Please move, or excuse me, so she would not offend the enchanted beings. Once she tripped over a giant turtle and she thought of turning back. But she had to get to the spring that night or else wait another year. She touched her face; she would not wait.

She pushed forward until she came to a stream. After wading across, the girl followed the flowing water to a clearing. She quickened her steps — beyond was the spring. The distant gurgling of water seemed to repeat her name: Marta-Marta-Marta. She ran to the spring and gazed at the silvery water that frothed and bubbled in a tireless dance. If she were only beautiful, she would be tireless when dancing all night. Kneeling down, she scooped up water — it was cool. She took a sip — it was sweet like sugar cane juice. She waited for something to happen, some change in her, but she only heard the grunting of wild beasts in the bushes. The girl stroked her face once more — she was the same Marta with plump cheeks. The same plain face. Sighing, she thought of returning home to her parents and to her sister who would be May Queen.

She was standing up when she caught sight of a figure. Gasping, she hid behind the banana trees and observed a young man, perhaps a boy still, clad only in a colorful loin cloth. Carrying a hatchet in one hand and a gold chalice in the other, he walked with bold strides across the field and placed the two items in the middle of the clearing. He stared at them and mumbled a few words, which she could not understand. The man-boy started chanting a low mournful sound while shuffling around the two objects.

Biting her lower lip, the girl remained silent. When he stopped, she said, "So you took the chalice. Why would a jeweler's son steal a gold chalice?"

Her voice echoed through the forest and the boy turned around and around to find her. She laughed and stepped out under the moonlight. Her laughter trembled all around them.

"What are you doing here?" he asked, trying to hide his nakedness.

"The spring," she answered, pointing her chin toward the bubbling water.

"Ah, yes, the magic spring. Last year, I drank some spring water after Mama — " he paused.

"Last year your mother died."

"Yes."

"And?" she prodded.

"You know what happened. The whole town spoke of nothing else for weeks."

"She died and was buried outside the cemetery."

"Yes," he said. "The old friar who smells like a goat refused her Christian burial. She was buried in unhallowed ground."

"Was she Christian? If not she will burn in hell or spend the rest of eternity in limbo," she said.

"She was! She was Christian — and Itneg. She worshipped a Creator as her ancestors did. As my ancestors did."

"Are you now an Itneg warror, jeweler's son?" she asked.

He nodded and straightened his back so his brown skin shimmered. "And I have avenged her humiliation," he said, glaring at the gleaming chalice.

She sat down next to the chalice and hatchet. "How does revenge feel, Itneg warrior?" She studied the muscles etching his young body. He squatted down beside her and together they looked up at the blood-red moon.

"Revenge is like eating a basket of tamarinds. First it is sweet, but it sours swiftly." He sighed and through the silence, they heard the snorting of boars darting about.

She laughed. "Does your stomach ache then?"

He paused and stared at her. "I ache all over."

She understood that he was afraid and said, "I'll return the chalice. I'll say I found it on the seashore. They will not think that I took it. Go home now."

"Yes, Papa will be looking for me. I'm all he has left."

The girl got up, shook the dry grass from her skirt, and picked up the gold chalice. "Goodbye for now, Itneg warrior," she said.

He looked at her. The moon streamed down and around her like endless silk, and he caught his breath — "You are beautiful," he finally said.

She tossed her head and gave a silvery laugh as she raced down the trail to town.

THE BALETE TREE

AFTER BREAKFAST, Tiya Remia started. "Pay attention, Milagros," she ordered. "A woman must know how to handle an egg properly — like this." She cracked a brown egg and with a slight twist, dropped the bright yellow yolk and slimy egg white into the blue enameled bowl.

"Save the shells for the orchids," her aunt continued as she threw the shells into a bucket and wiped her hands gingerly on her lace-trimmed apron. She moved in precise economical movements.

"It's a simple thing, but there are disastrous women out there who demolish the yolk or shatter the shells so you end up with shells in your food."

"Yes, Tiya," Milagros replied, but her mind was on the tadpole that had sprouted little legs. It was in a jar under her bed. Last week her older brother Melchor had caught hundreds of tadpoles at the river and had given her a jarful. Most of them had died and only a handful remained. This morning she discovered that one of them had grown legs.

"Cooking, cleaning, sewing, embroidery — all these are of utmost importance. If you expect to marry well, you must master these womanly arts." Tiya Remia beat the eggs vigorously with a fork. Her lips were two thin lines and she had a fuzzy mustache. Her sparse dark hair was pulled back in a tight bun at her nape. She wore black, as Milagros did, because they were in mourning. Milagros' grandmother — Tiya Remia's mother — had been eating pickled pig snout when she choked and died ten months ago.

"Milagros, I know what you are thinking, 'Well, why isn't Tiya Remia married if she knows everything?'" She paused, her face softening. "I had many suitors. There was one in particular ..." Her voice trailed and her face hardened once more as she continued "... but, well, as God would have it, I have been called to a life of single blessedness. And a good thing for you. Mama — may she rest in peace — spoiled you. No doubt she felt sorry that you have no mother. And your father is far too busy to attend to you. When I moved in, you had lice ..." Tiya Remia raised her thin shoulders and shivered, "... a mayor's daughter with lice! And you hang around with the boys near the balete tree. Just like a wild thing! A wild thing!"

Milagros pulled her braids and studied the ends, searching for the pearly white nits, remembering the burning sensation of kerosene on her scalp and the irritation of the fine comb running through her hair repeatedly. She thought of Melchor who had raced out of the house after breakfast to play and she felt her stomach grow sour.

The cook, fat and sweaty Menggay, had forgotten to stop by Agustina's place. Milagros was glad when Tiya Remia told her to run over and pick up two dozen chorizos. "And don't tarry," her aunt said. "That woman is bad influence altogether. Why a doctor's wife continues with this sausage business, I'll never understand. And I cannot comprehend her insistence on running around with her long hair flying all over the place. It is unseemly. And her American husband ... well, I've never liked their kind. As far as I'm concerned, they can all go back to Kansas, or wherever they come from."

Milagros skipped down the cobblestones toward the river. It was only midmorning but the sun was already scorching the narrow, winding streets of Ubec. When the sea breeze blew, dust rose, whirled around, then settled once more.

She was sweating hard and felt her cotton blouse sticking to her back. To catch some shade, she ran from tree to tree.

It was cooler by the river and she slowed down to observe the laundry women beating the clothes on the rocks. She recalled the story about Agustina's mother and the river spirit who sired her. Tiya Remia said Agustina had horns like Satan, that she was a Jezebel, but Milagros was fond of the vivacious woman. Her husband, the American doctor, had golden hair on his head and even on his arms. He was learned, often talking about germs and modern medicine. Milagros hoped he would be home so she could ask him how the tadpole grew legs.

Agustina's house stood near where the river and sea collided and formed whirlpools. It was a two-story house with capiz-shell windows, carved wooden balconies, and a scarlet bougainvillea vine that crawled up one wall and spilled over the tiled roof.

Agustina, her daughter, and her husband were not home. After paying the cook for the chorizos, Milagros stayed to watch her kill a chicken. The cook wrestled with the chicken, pinning its wings to the side until she held it firmly. Then she took the machete and with one stroke, cut off the head. Blood spurted out of the neck. With a sudden burst of energy, the headless chicken fluttered out of the cook's hands and ran around the yard.

Milagros hiked her skirt up, ready to chase the chicken, but hesitated knowing Tiya Remia would be displeased to see blood all over her. The sight of blood distressed her.

The chicken flailed its wings as it ran aimlessly around, knocking over a huge clay jug, trailing blood wherever it went. At last, the chicken collapsed. The cook picked it up, dunked it in a cauldron of boiling water and proceeded to pluck its feathers. Milagros picked up a brown feather and reflected on how swiftly all that had happened. A little while ago, the chicken had been alive, now it was featherless and gutted, ready to be made into soup. Her grandmother too had been alive one moment, then dead the next.

Melchor with three boys were huddled together on the riverbank. The biggest boy was boasting about having seen the *agta* last night. He said he walked through the cemetery to the balete tree and saw the enormous black giant sitting on the top branch, puffing away on his cigar.

The boys were impressed, and Melchor said he went to the balete tree at siesta time and also saw the *agta*. Milagros glanced at him, knowing Tiya Remia did not allow them near the tree. Her aunt had such a dislike for the tree and had often spanked them with her slipper for playing in the area. "Stay-away-from-the-balete-tree," she intoned as she hit them in rhythm to her words.

Milagros gazed across the river to the cemetery and the balete tree on the riverbank. The tree was the oldest in town, huge with sprawling branches and thick roots that swelled around the base. The *agta*, an enchanted being, lived in the tree. A long time ago, the parish priest had wanted the tree chopped down because its roots were destroying the cemetery walls. Overnight, the priest had died mysteriously in his sleep. And once, a servant girl who walked by the tree daily, was snatched by the *agta* who had taken a liking to her. The girl was never seen again.

When she had the chance, Milagros told the boys about her tadpole with little legs. The three boys ignored her and jumped into the river. Melchor said he'd look at her tadpole, but he turned and joined the boys on their way to the balete tree.

It was gone. Her jar with tadpoles was gone. She checked under her bed and scoured her room carefully. She could not find it. Running into the kitchen, she asked the maid where the jar was. Just then Tiya Remia walked in and shivered. "Slimy, disgusting creatures," she said. "I got rid of them." Milagros went to her room and wept.

Later she watched the gecko climb up the wall to the ceiling right above her head. The crickets outside were humming. The yard was full of them and when the sun set, they made their sawing sounds. The gecko had bulging eyes and a protruding stomach. It looked a bit like her tadpole with legs.

She was lying there, holding her small blanket that used to be yellow, green, and orange. Now it was worn around the edges and the brilliant colors had faded. Since her grandmother died and Tiya Remia moved in, Milagros slept with it every night.

She was comparing the size of the gecko with the faster-moving gray lizards when it fell right on her mosquito net, above her face. Without the net it would have landed right on top of her. She jerked and shouted. No one came. Her father was in Manila; Melchor was out playing. Tiya Remia was in the kitchen scolding the servants.

The gecko scampered away. Milagros hugged her blanket. The windows were open and the night breeze blew her net gently. The wind seeped through her net, caressing her face until she fell asleep.

Dragging the wooden rake methodically, the gardener gathered leaves and twigs into a pile. He made a bonfire that flared then settled into mesmerizing glowing embers. Thin ribbons of gray smoke trailed upward and diffused into the afternoon sky.

"Thank San Antonio he got around to doing that," Tiya Remia said as she slapped a mosquito on her arm.

"The smoke will get rid of the bugs, Tiya," Milagros answered as she struggled to make another cross-stitch on her sewing sampler. Her aunt wanted her to finish the sampler — which she had been working on for months — so she could start embroidering her own mantle.

"A woman is judged by her future mother-in-law by the quality of her needlework," Tiya Remia grumbled as she carefully inspected the sampler. She sighed, showing dissatisfaction at the irregular stitches. "Milagros, you must concentrate on your needlework, housework, cooking, rather than your tadpoles and God-knows-what-else."

Milagros studied her sampler thinking it looked just fine when Melchor, who was on bamboo stilts, doddered by. Distracted, she pricked her finger. She squeezed it and watched the round drop of blood form. Then she sucked her finger, surprised at how salty her blood tasted.

"You've hurt yourself," Tiya Remia said. "I abhor the sight of blood." Shivering, she turned away. She was quiet for a long while then said, "Well, let's rest awhile." Her aunt put her crocheting hook and spool of thread down. "Why don't you come with me and I'll show you something?" she suggested.

Milagros followed her to her room where her aunt opened a handsome carved camphor chest. A musty pungent smell filled the room. Tiya Remia removed a white gown, which she laid on her bed. The dress was made of fine piña fiber, with exquisite embroidery of flowery designs on the skirt and butterfly sleeves.

Her aunt's face beamed and her voice took on a dreamy quality. "Take a look at that stitchery," she said. "The famous modiste, Pacita Alesna, made this for me. She used silk thread and real pearls from Jolo. She charged me three hundred pesos, which was an outrageous sum then. It still is. But my fiancé insisted. He was a poet and a revolutionary. Isn't that the silliest thing you've heard? He was pale and thin and trembled when he was near me. Well ... but ... of course there was no wedding. But it is still a beautiful *terno* and it still fits me perfectly."

Milagros watched Tiya Remia's fingers travel slowly over the fine embroidery. There was a distant look in her eyes, a kind of wildness mixed with sadness.

"It is perfect craftmanship," her aunt concluded, as she carefully folded the white goen and returned it to the trunk.

She waited until the house was quiet, then waited some more. Quietly, she crept out of the house. In the streets, she listened for the night watchman and hid behind the bushes when he walked by. Some dogs barked at her as she hurried across the bridge and walked to the cemetery. The moon was large and bright and she could see the crumbling crypts and the white crosses on the ground. When she heard a weeping sound, she crossed herself and held her breath. She listened carefully and was relieved that it was only the sea breeze whistling through the crypts.

As she passed by her family mausoleum, she said a quick prayer for her grandmother. At the end of the cemetery, to her right, against crumbling cemetery walls, stood the balete tree. It was truly enormous and luminous under the moonlight. Four strong branches sprouted from the trunk and these forked into smaller branches. They sprawled outward giving the impression that they could carry the sky if it fell down.

Her breath quickened and her knees shook as she approached it. She searched the tree. When the wind blew, the leaves trembled and the branches shook. The quivering shadows appeared like a strange face or an arm. Blood rushed to her head and her heart pounded against her ribs.

The sound of splashing from the river startled her. River spirits, she thought. Milagros stepped over thick roots that pushed up the dank earth. She touched the rough bark timidly. Then she started climbing. Higher and higher she went until she reached the top. The sounds were clearer now. Low voices, soft laughter, water scattering. She sat on the branch and looked at the river expecting to see enchanted beings. She saw only Agustina, with her flowing dark hair, and her golden-haired husband frolicking in the water under the full moon.

The morning sun warmed her arm then her face. She covered her face with the pillow and tried to stay asleep but she heard kitchen sounds and Tiya Remia's high-pitched voice berating the cook: "The proper household must use fresh carabao's milk and not these newfangled American canned things."

Milagros listened for a while. Then she sat up and decided she'd go to the river that day to catch some tadpoles.

FRIDAY EVENING AT THE SEASHORE

PADRE ZOBEL LOCKED the rectory and, leaving the center of town, headed toward the seashore. He was a young Spaniard from the coastal village of Mojacar and he felt a special bond with the sea. It made his soul echo; it was home.

He was an athletic man and as he walked, he swung his arms around and shrugged his shoulders to loosen his taut muscles. He had been sitting, hearing confessions for four hours and he was weary. A zealous man, he suffered with his parishioners the guilt, shame, and pain as they mumbled their sins in the dark confessional. True, he also felt the sense of release, of joy, when their sins were absolved, but hearing confessions wrung his spirit. Other priests had advised him not to be so involved, but Padre Zobel could not help himself.

That Friday afternoon, another thought preoccupied him. He was concerned about a girl from his parish. Ligaya often attended the six o'clock Mass and Wednesday novenas to our Lady of Perpetual Succor. In his two years in Ubec, Ligaya had never missed Friday confessions until that day. He smiled to himself recalling her concerns: I was distracted during Mass, I was late for the novena. He had often wanted to assure her that her sins were hardly those at all. Such an endearing child, he thought. But recently there had been mention of a man, and she seemed flustered and withdrawn.

Ligaya involved with a man — it was disturbing.

It was almost suppertime. The tropical sun was dropping slowly and fishing boats that dotted the sea were returning home. He picked up a blue starfish stranded on a sandbar and threw it into the water. Then he sat on a coconut tree that had fallen from a past typhoon, and gazed at Ubec's bleached sugary sand and the frothy waves that curled up to the shore.

He sighed, absorbing the tranquility. In Mojacar, the beach had been rockier, more coarse, and the Mediterranean had been rougher and colder. But it was the same tangy sea breeze. He closed his eyes and took deep breaths. He pictured Mojacar with its whitewashed Moorish houses cascading down the hills. His home had been on the highest hill, and from his bedroom window, he used to see the flattop roofs, the ancient winding paths, and the sparkling sea.

When he opened his eyes, he saw the figure of a woman in the distance. "Ana Maria," he shouted, then wondered why he had called out his cousin's name. The line the woman cut against the horizon must have reminded him of his cousin — graceful, well-shaped, pleasing to the eye.

The woman turned his way. She hesitated and started walking the opposite direction. Then she stopped, turned, and walked toward Padre Zobel. He was surprised and pleased that it was Ligaya.

"Good evening, Padre," she said in that soft trembly voice. She was blushing.

"Ah, child, what are you doing here?"

"Just walking and thinking, Padre."

She stood there, eyes downcast, with an uncertain air so he said, "Sit down. Come, sit down."

Her skirt rustled as she sat on the log beside him. Her back was straight, her hands folded together like those of a schoolgirl.

"Walking and thinking," she repeated. She had a sprig of sampaguita flowers in her hair and the sweet scent filled the air around them.

"Were you sick today, child?"

She shook her head. "No ... well ... I helped Mama with the baking. The Mayor has a dinner tomorrow and the tortas and the mamons are tedious to make."

"Ah, I have been worried. You have never missed Friday confessions."

She blushed once more, her bronze skin turning a deep coral hue. She stared at her bare feet and wrapped her arms around herself. She took a deep breath, shivering slightly, and started to say something but hesitated.

"Something is bothering you?" he asked, feeling protective. How very much like Ana Maria's her mannerisms were. Ana Maria used to blush and hide her face behind her fan when embarrassed.

"Do you know what my name means, Padre?" Ligaya asked.

"Joy, is that right?"

"Yes, but I have never felt more joyless in my entire life," she whispered with pain in her voice.

She looked forlorn, so helpless, and he felt moved. "You had mentioned a man. Is it because of him?" he prodded.

She did not answer but studied her feet as they poked and dug into the white sand. Her silence gave him a sense of dread. He knew that her mother, a widow, was busy with her catering business.

"Perhaps there is no one to confide in," Padre Zobel said. "If you are involved ... that is, sometimes it happens that a girl finds herself ..."

He hesitated and she looked at him questioningly. "That is, a girl may be in a difficult situation and not have anyone to turn to."

"Difficult, Padre?"

"That is, with child."

Her head jerked up, her eyes widened as she stared briefly at him. "He doesn't even ..." then she stopped, lowered her gaze, and gave a soft laugh. She shook her head and stared ahead. He could see her perfect profile and the dark hair in a bun with the star-shaped flowers woven in. It was a lovely face; in a few years this child would be a beautiful woman.

Far away the sun touched the sea and the sky was splashed with red and purple. A solitary boat sliced across the horizon. The enchantment of the moment brought another memory to Padre Zobel — Ana Maria in the deep water with seaweed entangled around her legs. He had been a champion swimmer and brashly he swam the choppy water to help his cousin. She had flung her arms around his neck and he had removed the snakelike vines. Ana Maria had clung on while he swam back to the shore.

Ligaya's voice brought him back to the present. "In a way I am deeply involved."

"Yes?" he asked, but she became quiet. He grew embarrassed for having brought up such an intimate matter. But it happened often: young girls getting pregnant; rushed marriages. Often the girls were sent to another town until the child was born. Then the baby was raised by relatives or given to an orphanage. This occurred all too often and he could not dismiss this possibility even with Ligaya. Why, Ana Maria had gotten involved with the English merchant who fortunately had been willing to marry her.

"He has possessed me," Ligaya said. She put her palms together as if in prayer. "I think about him constantly. When the cock crows at dawn and I awaken, he is on my mind. At the market or while polishing the floors, I think of him. Always. I struggle to put him out of my thoughts, but I cannot help myself."

Ah, a young girl's infatuation, surmised Padre Zobel. He wanted to smile, but appearing serious and choosing his words, he said: "These feelings are normal. One must pray. Chastity you understand is a virtue. If the boy loves you, he will respect your wishes."

She hesitated. "He is … the problem is …" then sighed deeply. She bent over and removed the tortoise shell comb from her hair. Long hair tumbled to her waist. The tiny white sampaguita flowers were almost blinding against that mass of black hair.

Turning, she fixed wide somber eyes on him. A tender wisp of hair blew across her face. "Have you ever felt so passionately about someone?" she asked.

Her words startled him but he caught himself and decided to best way to guide this young girl was to be honest.

"The young have intense emotions. I loved once, yes, but God called her to another life, and I, to mine. Continue praying. Say the rosary and attend the novenas. God will give you strength."

Ligaya cocked her head to one side and with a slanted smile said, "I stopped praying because of him. I think of him and wonder how his mouth would feel against mine. Would his lips be soft, or would they feel like the back of my hand?" She brushed the back of her right hand against her lips and closed her eyes slowly. "I wonder how his kiss would feel. I have never kissed a man before. I wonder how his body would feel against mine."

Padre Zobel had never heard such passion and he felt an odd sensation in the pit of his stomach. "Perhaps," he suggested, "marriage is the best answer."

"He is not free to marry."

Ah, he thought sadly, at least in Ana Maria's case, the man had been unmarried. "Does this man know about your feelings?"

She shook her head. "No, no, he doesn't know." Before he could say anything, she rose and said, "I must go." Then she departed, leaving his soul with strange echoes.

Padre Zobel studied the figure walking away, her waist-length hair flowing around her. There was just enough light to see the woman's silhouette against the dying horizon. Padre Zobel caught his breath — what will happen to her, he wondered. He sat there, pondering her, even as darkness came.

MIRACLE AT SANTO NIÑO CHURCH

BEFORE THE SUN rose above the tiled roof of the ancient church, Tecla heard dragging sounds. She rubbed the sleep from her eyes and in the semidarkness made out the figure of a man with a bayonet walking toward her. She felt her liver grow cold. He had found her after all, and he would kill her just as he had killed Marcelo and the children. She was lying on a flattened-out cardboard box at the church entrance, and holding her breath, she plastered herself against the church door. Perhaps she would blend in with the carved saints on the massive wooden doors.

"Manang Tecla, wake up," the man said. He stood just three yards away from her. She rubbed her eyes again and squinted. It was Pedring, the street vendor, carrying some poles. Tecla realized it was Sunday and Pedring was setting up his stall. She laughed softly to herself.

"What's so funny?" Pedring asked kindly as he put the poles on the ground and placed a square plywood on top. He laid rosaries, religious medals and prayers books on his makeshift table.

Tecla sat up and wrapped her dusty black dress around her legs. "For a while there, I thought you were a Japanese soldier."

"Not me, just a poor man trying to make centavo. The

wife's pregnant again. You'd better get up. I saw Father Martin opening up the church." He offered his hand. She looked at him sideways and smiled coyly.

"C'mon, old woman. I don't have all morning. This place will be bustling soon."

She scowled. Old woman, indeed. Didn't he know that she was once a beauty queen? Miss Ubec, the gold sash across her chest had said. Her float had been decorated with rosal, jasmine, and dama de noche flowers. The profusion of scents and colors had filled her senses. A real fountain had spouted water below her throne. She grabbed Pedring's hand and got up. She shook her dress and dust billowed around her and fell like heavy fog. Tecla took the tortoise shell comb from her head, twirled her long white hair into a bun and shoved the comb back to hold it in place.

The church bells chimed a melancholy "Silent Night." With surprising clarity, she remembered that it was the eighth of December and the birthday of Marcelo. She walked around the stone church to the servants' quarters where she used the smelly latrine that was swarming with flies.

Later, she rummaged through a pile of trash until she found a rusty tin can. Walking to the front of the church, she started to leave the church grounds when a young girl stopped her. "Wait, Manang," she called. "Here's a hardboiled egg and pan de sal. Father Martin said to give these to you." Tecla took the food and stuffed it in her right pocket. The front of her faded, sheared black skirt had two large pockets. From the other pocket, she took out a pair of blue knitted booties. She studied these for a while, then put them back.

After the young girl left, Tecla stood under the carved wrought iron gate, trying to remember what it was she had to do. The blistering tropical sun was up and beggars and hawkers rushed past her to claim areas next to the church walls and under the cool shade of sprawling acacia trees.

She retraced her steps, back to the latrine and the garbage. She was shaking her head, looking at the rusty tin can when she remembered. Tecla chuckle softly, thinking how silly she was to have forgotten.

Holding the rusty tin can in front of her, she passed the sour, grimy woman who laid a skin-and-bones baby on newspapers next to the church gate. The woman placed a chipped plate next to the sleeping infant and she scattered five coins on the plate. She sat down with the hard look of resignation.

As Tecla walked down the street, rainbow-colored jeepneys — blaring multi-noted horns — drove past her, leaving clouds of dust and exhaust fumes. She wrinkled her nose at the smell. When she saw the red, green and gold shimmering garlands that decorated the department stores, she clapped her hands. She smiled at the paper star lanterns that decorated the slum houses. Traffic was heavy on M.J. Cuenco Avenue because the horse of a *tartanilla* stopped in the middle of the street to urinate. The half-naked children on the sidewalks pointed and laughed heartily and Tecla laughed with them.

Near the corner sari-sari store, she saw three boys pinching off the lower bodies of black ants. She raised her arms and howled at them. The boys scattered, then regrouped and followed her for half a block, chanting, "Cra-zy woman, cra-zy woman." She looked down at her calloused feet. She was barefoot, her toes spread out, deformed. Her feet plodded with quick determination until at last she reached the old cemetery.

Thick cadena de amor vines crawled and entwined on the cemetery walls. She snapped off some branches with pink and white flowers. Tecla put them in the rusty tin can, then went to a dripping fire hydrant and filled the can with water.

She proceeded to a crumbling mausoleum, stopping in front of three niches with fading inscriptions:

Marcelo Banaga, d. Jan. 6, 1945;

Josefa Banaga, d. Jan. 6, 1945;

Agapito Banaga, d. Jan. 6, 1945.

"It's your birthday again, Marcelo," she said aloud as she put the flowers in front of his niche. "I'll light a candle for all of you later."

She cleaned each niche, brushing off the cobwebs and crumbled plaster. She pulled nearby weeds and broke off the vines that threatened to cover the tombs.

When she finished, she squatted in front of the tombs. She took the egg from her pocket and cracked it on a nearby tombstone. She was peeling the egg when she saw a mangy, pregnant bitch cowering behind the tombstone. The dog wagged her tail timidly and looked straight into Tecla's eyes. "Poor creature," she muttered as she gave the egg to the dog.

She watched the mutt eat the egg, then she took the pan de sal from her pocket and broke it into four pieces. She put a piece in front of each niche and she ate the last one. Tecla had no teeth so she sucked and gummed the roll until it was gone. In a little while, she said, "I have to go back to church. I haven't checked the boy yet. It's Maria's day today and I think the miracle will be today. It was a year ago when she made the promise. She touched the inscribed names gently and left the cemetery.

She took the long route back to church, past Slapsy Maxie's bar near the pier, where the ugly prostitute worked. Once a month, the girl went to confession and she always looked for Tecla to give her money. Wearing a bright red or orange dress, the girl would smile but on her ugly face it looked like a grimace. Tecla couldn't find her. Only the tired-looking madam with smeared makeup barked at the servant boy to sweep the patio carefully.

Pedring greeted her by asking her to pick two lottery tickets for him: Tecla pondered on the tickets, finally choosing numbers with six, three and one. "Fifty-fifty if I win, Manang Tecla. *Lintik*, I need to win. The wife's going to have another brat," Pedring said as he paid the hare-lipped ticket vendor.

Tecla inspected the colorful wares displayed on the stalls. There were religious objects, clothes, rice and corn cakes wrapped in banana leaves. There were toys, too, her favorite being the plastic swimming dog. The vendor wound it, put it in a basin of water and the dog's giant ears did the paddling.

"Want to buy something, ma'am?" How about this medal of Santa Ana, blessed by the Pope?" a woman called out to her.

"Leave her alone," Pedring said and Tecla caught him pointing to his forehead and making circular movements with his finger. "Ever since her family died," he whispered.

"Oh," the woman said and looked at Tecla curiously.

Tecla glared at Pedring. Her blood boiled when people said she was crazy. Didn't they know she had been a doctor's wife? She once had servants, a nice house; she had run a smooth household for her husband and children. The image of their dead bodies came to her again. They had been sleeping when she left and she had not said goodbye to them. She had not kissed them goodbye. It turned out her cousin hadn't needed her because the midwife was in her barrio. If Tecla had been home, she would have fought like a wild boar until the damnable Japanese cringed in terror and fled. She had tried to blow life back into them but their bodies remained cold and stiff; the blood of their bodies, crusty. All she had now, the only one who understood, who forgave her, was Maria. Tears trickled down, making little crooked paths on her dusty cheeks.

She made her way to the stand with the vigil candles. She reached deep into her pocket and took out the coin that the ugly prostitute had given her. Tecla put it into the collection box and lit a candle. The flame flickered and danced like a firefly. Once, she had seen a bush covered with fireflies and it looked like an enormous enchanted ball. She gasped at the memory and placed her tongue against her palate. She threw her head back and made a trilling sound. Her feet started shuffling as she began to dance. Churchgoers paused and pointed at her, but she didn't mind. She was in perfect harmony, dancing her prayer to Maria.

After a timeless period, her legs gave way and she fell into a tired heap near the candles. A drop of wax fell on her brown, gnarled hand and she jerked back in pain. It occurred to her that this was a divine sign that today would be the day of fulfillment. Father Martin helped her to her feet. "Be careful,

Tecla. You'll hurt yourself," he said and walked away.

The church was cool and dark and smelled of incense and melted wax. A Mass was starting and people filled the pews and stood along the aisles. Ignoring the people who pressed against her, Tecla knelt in the middle aisle and started walking on her knees toward the altar. She prayed, "*Santa Maria, madre de Dios* ..." until she reached the communion rail.

She stopped and gazed at the back wall that was filled with statues. There were four dozen all in all — Tecla had counted them many times — and in the center was the statue of the Santo Niño. The Child Jesus was about as big as her arm, with a scarlet cloak and a gold crown. She narrowed her eyes to study his cloak hem. It was clean and dry; Tecla was pleased. It was only because of her militant guard that the Santo Niño stayed inside the church. She had heard the stories about the Santo Niño roaming the city at night. In the morning, people said, the friars would find the ancient statue muddy and dirty from his promenade.

"*Libera nos a malo*," Father Martin said. Tecla went to Maria's altar at the back of the church and gazed lovingly at her statue. She was dressed in white with a blue sash around her waist. Her long curly hair peeked out of her white veil. Her face shone with love and understanding. Maria's son, after all, had been killed by soldiers.

Tecla told her that the Santo Niño was fine, that he had not wandered around Ubec. No telling what would happen to a mere child like that, walking the streets at night. There were women in tight dresses with Norwegian sailors doing God-knows-what in bars and massage parlors. Many houses reeked of opium. The incessant clicking of ivory mahjong pieces echoed through the narrow streets of Ubec.

The coolness of the church gave way to an oppressive heat. Tecla wiped off the beads of perspiration that sprouted on her forehead. "Please move," a woman said. "Our granddaughter has to be near us. She's sick, you see." Tecla opened her eyes and saw a plump woman in rich clothing and a thin old man. She closed her eyes once more and centered herself on her prayers.

Father Martin's sermon was long and the heat filled the musty corners of the church. Tecla was wiping her salty sweat from her eyes when she heard a woman exclaim, "*Madre mia,* she's fainted!" Then, "Jesus! She's not breathing; she's dead!" The plump woman stood there, one hand to her throat, staring at a girl who lay in a white heap near her feet. The girl was around sixteen, pale and thin.

From some corner of Tecla's mind, a memory surfaced. She went near the girl. The plump woman screamed and clutched her throat tighter, but Tecla continued with what she knew she had to do. She looked at the girl's face. White and still, just like her husband and children had been. She passed her hand in front of the girl's nose and there was no breath. Tecla pushed the girl's chin back and forced her mouth open. She put her mouth on hers, stubbornly resisting the clawing hands on her shoulders and hair. Tecla blew air until she felt the girl's chest go up. She pulled away and her chest went down. She continued doing this until the girl's chest rose and fell on its own. Only then did Tecla allow the people to pull her away.

"She's dead. The dirty beggar killed her," the plump woman wailed.

"No, no, she's all right," the thin old man said as he helped the girl to her feet. The girl leaned against her grandfather, one hand to her forehead. She wore a pure white dress with a blue ribbon around her waist. Her hair was long and curly. When the girl smiled at Tecla, Tecla thought — just for a brief moment — that this was Maria's apparition. The miracle.

The plump woman crushed the girl to her enormous bosom. People crowded around them until Tecla could not see the girl. Tecla chuckled to herself. How could she have mistaken the girl for Maria? What a silly thought. She went back to Maria's altar, counted the number of flowers in the huge bouquets, and wondered when Maria's promise of a miracle would be fulfilled.

WAITING FOR PAPA'S RETURN

WHEN REVEREND Mother Superior tells Remedios her father died, all she can think is how ugly the nun looks. Remedios stares at the mustache fringing the nun's upper lip; Reverend Mother Superior stares back with pale watery eyes.

"This morning, child. Heart attack," the nun says.

In the distance the three o'clock bell rings as if repeating the nun's words. It is an October Thursday, warm and humid. The sound stays with Remedios as the nun brings her to the chapel. "Let us pray so your father will go straight to heaven," she whispers. They kneel on the front pew and Remedios closes her eyes. The ringing that echoes in her head fades and she hears her father's voice loud and clear: I'll be back in two weeks.

She clings to those words, mulling over them. I'll-be-back-in-two-weeks. That means next week because Mama and Papa have already been gone for a week. She pictures her father with his oval face, his gold rimmed glasses, and his balding head. Leaning on his cane, he asked, "What do you want me to bring?"

"Mama says she'll buy me shoes, clothes, candies, and chocolates."

"But what do you want?" his gentle voice prodded.

"A walking doll and a tea set like Mildred's. Not the

48

plastic tea set, I want the kind that breaks."

"All right," he replied, tousling her dark hair. "I'll scour all of Hong Kong and I'll bring you your doll and tea set."

Those words her father said and he never lies. Remedios is confused: Reverend Mother Superior is the most important person in school and she doesn't lie either. She must have made a mistake. Papa and Mama will be back next week from their vacation.

Remedios thinks things over, trying to find a reason for this misunderstanding. Was it because she and Mildred giggled in church at the fat woman singing in a warbling voice? Mildred elbowed her in the ribs and they were bad, no doubt about it, snickering in the back row instead of paying attention to Father Ruiz's novena.

The chapel smells of melted wax, and when Remedios opens her eyes, she studies the bleeding Jesus nailed to the cross. "I'm sorry for having been bad," she prays over and over, until Reverend Mother Superior stands up and says, "Your aunt is picking you up, child."

They find Tiya Meding in the office. She is wearing a brown dress; her face is pale, her eyes, pink-rimmed. "Poor, poor child," she mumbles. In the car she looks at Remedios in a way that makes Remedios think her aunt is trying to discover something in her — and Remedios does not know what.

Feeling awkward, Remedios rolls down her window and watches the hawkers selling lottery tickets, boiled bananas and soft drinks. Her aunt delicately blows her nose and sniffles.

"Look, there's the woman in black, dancing in front of the church," Remedios points out.

"Crazy woman," Tiya Meding answers.

"Papa says she's pathetic."

"Pathetic, my food. She's as loony as they come."

Remedios keeps quiet; pathetic is how her father describes the woman in black.

Her aunt's chauffeur — that is what Tiya Meding calls her driver — brings them to Vering the Dressmaker. Remedios is surprised that she will have a dress sewn, and she nods approvingly at the design: puffed sleeves, boat neck and shirred skirt.

"And pockets, two square pockets," Remedios says.

Vering sketches in the pockets.

"And I don't want this black cloth. Yellow organdy would be nicer."

The two women eye each other.

"But the dress has to be black," Tiya Meding insists.

"I don't like black. Papa says I look prettiest in yellow."

"The dress will be black, Remedios." Her aunt sets her jaw and Remedios knows there is no use arguing.

Before leaving the dressmaker's shop, Tiya Meding asks for pieces of black cloth the size of postage stamps, and she pins one on Remedios' blouse, right above her heart — a little bit of black cloth that flutters when the warm breeze blows.

At school she is the center of attraction, like the actress Gloria Romero or the one-eyed freak with the Chinese Acrobatic Troupe, stared at by everybody. When she picks up her schoolbag, the children glance curiously at her. The visitors streaming into Tiya Meding's house look at her, and when she and her aunt go to the funeral parlor and church "to make arrangements," people study her. Remedios feels as if her nose were growing from her forehead. Pairs of glassy eyes follow her around and she does not know what they want, how to escape them.

At her aunt's house, she tries to amuse herself by inspecting the numerous porcelain figures in the living room — pretty dainty women with ducks beside them, little angels kneeling down in prayer, but her aunt snaps: "Don't touch those. They're breakable." She goes to the piano and plays "Chopsticks," but her aunt lifts a reprimanding finger in the air. "The noise," she complains. Tiya Meding is on the phone and Remedios listens to her.

"Thank you," her aunt says. "Heart attack. Isn't that too bad? I warned my sister. An older man like that." Tiya Meding's diamond earrings dangle from her elongated ears and a huge diamond solitaire sparkles on her finger.

"Baubles," her father often says about Tiya Meding's jewelry. "She is a silly woman who likes baubles."

Remedios leaves the main house thinking to herself: Silly, silly woman. She goes to the dirty-kitchen and has a second lunch with the servants. Using her fingers, she makes a ball of rice and eats that with stewed fish. Later, she helps the cook peel cassava and grate coconuts.

"Your father was a good man," the cook says. "He made my son the foreman at the road construction."

"Yes," Remedios replies, "I can't wait until he comes home."

After speaking, she wonders why she said those words at all. She understands what Reverend Mother Superior said, what all the commotion is about, yet deep in the very core of her, she knows her Papa will return.

The kitchen is sooty and smells of grease and bay leaves. The cook, standing next to the huge wood-burning stove, looks at her. Remedios continues grating. She watches the curly slivers of white coconut meat fall into the basin. The kitchen smoke seems to engulf her and she feels warm. The pungent smell makes her temples throb. She begins to feel weak, just as she felt when her cousin told her she was adopted. He had lost in a game of checkers, and angrily, he told Remedios that her parents picked her up from a pile of trash, that she had been covered with fat flies. She did not cry; she crawled into bed to sleep off her tiredness. Her mother called the boy an idiotic pervert. Her father placed her on his knee.

"See this bump on my nose?" he said.

"Yes."

"Don't you have a bump on your nose like mine?" His warm finger traveled down her nose over the slight protrusion.

She nodded.

"That mean that you are my very own little girl. We didn't adopt you."

The darkness lifted, and the next time she saw her cousin, she stuck her tongue out at him. But now the tiredness stays and she drags around until bedtime. It seems she has just tucked the mosquito net under the mattress when she falls asleep and has a dream.

It is Sunday, and she, Mama and Papa are driving over bumpy, dusty roads to Talisay Beach. Remedios is happy because she enjoys clamming in the small inlet. But when they arrive, the sea is blood-red and smells foul. Remedios cries and her Papa asks why.

"Something terrible has happened," she says.

"It's all right," he answers. "I'm right beside you."

She dries her eyes and, noticing that the water has turned blue and the air is clean once more, laughs and hugs her Papa.

"Don't cry. It makes me sad," her father says in her dream.

She wakes to Tiya Meding's voice telling her the plane is arriving in less than an hour. Trying to get excited, she bathes with her aunt's Maja soap and dabs Joy perfume behind her ears. Like a sleepwalker, she puts on her new black dress, white socks, and black patent shoes. Remedios ties yellow ribbons at the ends of her braids, but Tiya Meding removes those. "Not for a year," she says.

Heavy-faced people wearing somber clothes crowd at the airport. They stare at Remedios and she tries hard to figure out what they want from her. She laughs. "I can hardly wait to see them," she exclaims in a high thin voice. Pairs of eyes follow her, letting go only when the noisy plane arrives with a loud screech. The special cargo plane stops near the terminal, and some men open the side doors and struggle to bring a casket down. When Remedios spots her mother walking down the ramp, she runs shouting, "Ma!" The mourners around her pause. "Ma, where's my walking doll and tea set?" Her aunt tells her to be quiet. "She's just a child," someone says. "Just a child."

Her mother appears dreary in her black dress — Remedios really hates that color — and she weeps constantly. She will not talk, will not tell Remedios that everything will be fine.

A hollow feeling roots inside Remedios and sometimes she feels like a conch shell sitting on the writing desk. Other times it seems she is hanging on a thin thread, like the gray spider that swings back and forth from the ceiling. She feels odd, as if waiting for something to happen so all the staring will end, so the strangeness that has invaded her life will disappear.

The next day there is a Mass, then the men carry the coffin to the funeral car, so black and slick. When it starts raining, people scramble for umbrellas or newspapers and they mutter: Ah, a good sign, heaven is weeping. She, Mama and Tiya Meding walk behind the funeral car to the old cemetery with gray crumbling crypts. Some women hold umbrellas over them to keep their heads dry. Remedios trudges along, splashing in puddles, watching the slum children playing in the rain.

At the cemetery, the men pick up the coffin, carry it to the family crypt, and open it. The priest sprinkles holy water inside. Her Mama, who emits wailing sounds and whose shoulders are shaking, bends over to kiss the man inside. Remedios has not looked, but she knows that a man is in there. She had heard people talking: "Looks like he's sleeping, doesn't he? They sure did a good job."

Her Mama turns to her and Remedios walks toward the casket. Tiptoeing, she peers in. The man's face is a waxy mask. He doesn't wear glasses and his tight little smile is a grimace. There is a smell like mothballs. Remedios feels faint. She wants to giggle, but stopping herself, she bends over and plants a kiss on the wax-man's cool cheek.

The men close the coffin and slide it into the crypt with a grating sound. There is a dull thud when the marble slab covers the niche, and briefly, Remedios feels a lurching inside her stomach. She closes her eyes and hears that voice loud and clear: I'll be back in two weeks. I'll bring you our doll and tea set.

When she opens her eyes and sees the mourners crying,

for just a brief moment, she understands that they want her to weep, that they have been waiting for her to cry. But soon she is thinking of dainty tea cups, the smooth feel of delicate china, the clinking sound as the cup hits the saucer. She is seeing her father smiling broadly as she hands him his cup, and they make a toast pretending to sip tea under the cool shade of the lush star apple trees.

THE BLUE-GREEN CHIFFON DRESS

SUMMER VACATION started off badly with my favorite guard dog getting killed. I was heading for the hammock with my *Lady Chatterley's Lover* tucked under my arm, and a plateful of green mangoes and a Coke in my hands when Sultan walked up to me, stiff and hostile. His eyes were giant marbles. I called him and he bared his teeth, growling a little. His mouth was foaming. I ran, sounding an alarm, and the next thing I knew one of the men shot him. I saw him writhing, blood gushing to the cracked brown earth. There was something other than blood that oozed out of his gut. I touched him; he was warm and became very still.

Sultan had been a sickly puppy. The servants had talked about drowning him but I took him under my care. He used to race to the gate when I arrived from school, and he'd jump up to lick my face. His death left me nauseous and sad.

To make me feel better, Mama took me to her couturier, who was famous in Ubec for his expensive high fashion clothes. We caught him peering out of his shop at the American soldiers walking by.

"That one looks like James Bond," he said, pinching my arm enthusiastically. "Oy, love those bushy eyebrows," he cooed with a roll of his eyes.

Eventually, he got around to me, scrutinized me and

said I had grown. He sketched a few dress designs and he and Mama discussed the drawings, material and cost while I roamed his shop.

I was studying his ready-made dresses, frowning at the price tags, when a blue-green chiffon dress caught my gaze. The color was stunning, bringing to mind the deepest part of the sea. The soft billowy cloth was draped across the bosom making a deep V-neckline. The skirt was generously gathered and flowed in the same draped effect.

I showed the dress to Mama who said it was too sophisticated for a teenager. The couturier prodded me to try on the dress.

"Go ahead, Gemma," he insisted, and to my mother in an admonishing tone, "This is 1965, we must keep up with the times."

Before entering the fitting room, I glanced at him gratefully, our eyes locking briefly.

The bodice was loose so I stuffed Kleenex to fill it out. It was an enchanting dress and even my mother begrudgingly agreed. The couturier gushed over the blue-green hue.

"It makes your skin glow," he said. "Put your hair up in a French twist. We'll have to take in the tucks at the bust. And please wear a good padded bra," he added.

My cousin Yolanda and I went through the definitions of kissing, French kissing, petting, and intercourse again. Our favorite pastime was locking ourselves in the bedroom, slapping on makeup and discussing sex.

"I still don't know exactly how it enters the woman's part," I said.

"*Idiota*, it just goes in," she replied in exasperation. She had this superior attitude since Tristan danced slow drag with her and became aroused — she said.

When our eyelashes were curved and stiff with mascara, we decided to iron our hair. We had read that it made your hair straighter and shinier. I spread my hair out on the board, warning her not to singe it. She lightly ran the iron over my hair, then I did hers. After, we swished our hair around our shoulders to see a difference.

"Manolette smiled at me at church yesterday," I announced. "He's so sexy, I think I'll make him Number Two.

We proceeded to work on our crush-lists, shuffling the names of the boys in order of their appeal. I demoted Mandy to Number Ten because he had gone out with Mercedes.

"They were necking. Why else do people park in Magellan Hills?" Yolanda said. "No big loss, Mandy has no imagination."

She added that her Number One was Ruy who claimed to have had an out-of-body experience. "At least Ruy has imagination," she insisted. "Who's your Number One?" she asked.

I told her it was Jose Marie, a senior engineering student —5'11", lean, intelligent, much older at twenty-one. I fancied myself IN LOVE with him and got sweaty palms when he danced with me

During the summer, Ubec was pleasant. It was not as humid as Manila because the cool sea breeze blew through the ancient acacia and flame trees. There was so much color at that time of year: the sparkling blue sea; the brilliant clear sky; lush hibiscus, begonias and fuchsias; and bountiful fruit — yellow-green custard apples, luscious red mangosteens, succulent pink tambis.

The days flowed with little care. In the evenings, we attended parties or watched stocky Basque players hit the balls at the Jai-a-lai. Sometimes we went to the Sand Trap Club to dance to Amapola's music. There were movies, swimming parties and afternoon gossip sessions. And there was smoke-filled Eddie's Log Cabin, owned by an expatriate New Yorker, where we had greasy American-style hamburgers.

Our routine was disrupted when one of the local girls, Elena, suddenly left for Hong Kong. In minutes, stories about her mysterious departure flew all over Ubec and continued flying for weeks. Her family insisted she needed extensive allergy tests. Gossip mentioned an illegal abortion and the American captain she had been dating.

Ubec's matrons immediately stepped up their campaign against the American soldiers from nearby Mactan Air Force Base. From their mahjong tables, they lectured: "*Madre mia*, stay away from those soldiers, you'll catch Vietnam Rose. They're trouble. Look what happened to Elena."

I had already heard World War Two stories about American G.I.'s spreading V.D., getting girls pregnant, ruining lives forever. We knew a girl who stood 5'9" — a giant to our eyes —with fair hair and skin. She stood out like an aberration beside the rest of us with our small frames, black hair and brown skin. "A G.I. baby," she was called behind her back.

"Stay away from those soldiers," the matrons scolded as they shuffled the ivory pieces.

We, good girls, stayed away.

We watched — from a distance — the dazed, short-cropped strangers wandering around our city. We made up stories: that one was a CIA-agent; that brunet was on R&R; the slight one with a nervous laugh was flying to Vietnam the next day on a bombing mission. We read about Diem, napalm, deforestation, and body counts. We saw photos of Buddhist monks burning in fierce self-immolation. We drove by the Base, saw the runway, tower, barracks, and the numerous planes. Several times a day, we listened to those planes flying overhead. We were scandalized by the shanties, claiming to be bars and massage parlors, which mushroomed all over the place. We clucked our tongues at the girls in tight colorful clothes who hung around with the soldiers.

We watched — from a distance.

Eventually, we tired talking about Elena's disgrace. I resumed my crush-list, with Jose Marie maintaining his Number One place. I was glad he was invited to my cousins's

End-of-Summer party. For days I fretted about the affair. I dieted, painted my nails pink, dyed my hair Jet Black with some cheap dye called Bigen that I later heard made some women blind.

On the night of the party, I stared at my blue-green dress as if it were some talisman. It would transform me into an enchantress, a goddess, and Jose Marie would be smitten and ask me to go steady with him. I kissed the back of my hand, imagining his lips on mine.

I tugged at my padded bra and put on the dress. I applied another layer of mascara and reddened my cheeks and lips. Then I slipped on my gold heels and studied myself in the mirror. I smiled, pleased with myself. Ordinarily I appeared average-looking with a pleasant round face — no bones to speak of, no strong facial characteristics that made people say: Oh, what pretty eyes, or, what a lovely mouth. Normally, I was just average. But that night, I actually looked beautiful. I was glad I had saved the dress all summer, for the right moment, for that night.

The party was slow. The band, called "The Magnificent Seven," was off-key and the boys stayed in the patio drinking San Miguels, Rum Cokes and a beer-gin-Coke concoction dubbed Virgin Coke. The girls were huddled in the living room — which served as the dance floor —gossiping about Carla and the two American soldiers with her.

"I didn't want to invite her but her mother and mine are second cousins," Yolanda explained.

"Papa's going to whip me when he hears about this," whined Dolores, whom we called Turtle Face.

"They're just sitting outside, not doing anything," I ventured.

"You will end up like Elena, Gemma," Turtle Face said. She stared at me. "So, that's your new dress by the famous Mario. By the way, where's Jose Marie?"

"He'll be here," I answered smugly, as I fussed with the

folds of my skirt.

"I heard he and Mercedes are parked up in Magellan Hills. That Mercedes can probably find her way to those hills blind." Dolores' turtle mouth twisted into a little smile.

In my mind, Jose Marie plummeted from Number One to about Number Twenty. I felt angry and humiliated, and I consoled myself by thinking he would surely go to hell for necking with that cheap Mercedes.

I was forcing a smile, trying to save face, when someone asked me to dance. The band was terrible, no one was dancing, and someone was asking me to make a spectacle of myself. I glared up and caught a flash of red hair and wide grin on an oval face. An American soldier.

The girls stared at us with unhinged mouths. I didn't know what to do so I got up to dance slow drag with the stranger. I thought I heard giggling in the room.

The American said something but the music was too loud. His mouth moved up and down, then he looked at me quizzically. I tapped my right ear and shrugged my shoulders. He tried once more and I heard, "... nice dress." Aside from Yolanda, he was the only person who had said my dress was nice. I smiled and he grinned wider. When the music ended, he walked me to my seat and left.

"What did the Americano say, Gemma? How'd it feel dancing with him?" Dolores asked.

I felt my chest constrict and I shouted, "Do I have to wash my hands so I don't catch anything deadly?" I waved my hands in front of her like a magician. "You are very provincial, do you realize that? Pro-vin-cial!" Then I left.

Outside I took a couple of deep breaths. I walked around the patio, past the boys who were getting drunk, until I found the American with another soldier and Carla.

Carla was wearing red with black net stockings. She worked as a secretary at the Base. We tagged her "fast" because she sported hickeys on her neck and dated American soldiers. It was rumored that she went "all the way." That night her date was Marcus, a good-looking Mexican-American. Peter, who had danced with me, was his friend.

When I joined them, Carla was showing Marcus how to do butterfly kisses. She shoved her face close to Marcus' cheek and batted her eyelashes rapidly. The two boys laughed and I laughed tentatively. They were drinking Virgin Cokes and I started drinking. I was sixteen, Jose Marie and Mercedes were necking, and I could drink if I wanted to. The iced sweet drink flowed down my throat.

I was feeling like a ripe mango when Carla started telling jokes.

"There was this bar called Sally's Legs," she related between giggles, "and one afternoon, a cop stopped a bum outside the bar, 'What are you doing here?' the cop asked. 'Waiting for Sally's Legs to open so I can have a drink.'"

They laughed while I tried to figure out the joke. Carla whispered an explanation in my ear and I laughed hysterically.

"Sally's Legs! I get it — Sally's Legs!"

"You're drunk," Carla said.

"Am I? Am I? I've never been drunk before," I said, still laughing.

But soon I felt depraved. I was drunk, sitting there with American soldiers, laughing at dirty stories. I was truly lost. Trying to look dignified, I sat up, pulled my skirt over my knees and folded my hands together. I studied the white-wrought iron chairs that we sat on, the jasmine vine covered with sweet-smelling flowers that climbed the trellis.

I watched the two soldiers whose arms and legs flopped all over the place. They were nice-looking, with strong bodies and boyish ways. I was surprised to realize that they were only a few years older than I. Still with milk on their lips, my mother would have said. They were talking now, their voices sounding like distant rain.

Peter said, "I'm tired. I just want to go home. First day in 'Nam I see these huge bundles stacked up near the plane and I lean against them. I'm smoking a cigarette like nothing's wrong, then later I find out those were dead bodies."

"Jeez!" exclaimed Marcus.

"No kidding, Marcus. Dead bodies."

"Peter, you've gotta be cool, man, or else you're not gonna make it," Marcus said. "You're feeling shitty 'cause you're going back tomorrow. Gotta be cool, man. Be like the NBC guy standing in front of a pile of gooks saying, 'This is Walter Bullshit reporting from Da Nang.'" He held an imaginary microphone in front of his mouth, as if he had actually seen this happen.

It's the waiting," Peter said. "It's draining. Like we're on a sweep last month and we're being real careful. You know somebody's going to get it and we watch our step carefully. Sweep and sweep, and you're waiting. You're so tight, then Boom! This poor guy beside me loses his leg. Just like that."

I became sad listening to them and my mind latched on to the image of Sultan's body on that dry earth. They could die too, I thought, on some brown earth someplace, far away from their homes.

"For me it's the food, man. Boy, do I miss Mama's carnitas and tamales. I'm sick of that shit they feed us." Marcus ran his tongue around his lips. "One more month, man, and I am through. I'm going home! I'm gonna stuff myself with enchiladas, rellenos, and I'm gonna cruise down Colorado Boulevard and just have a good time, you know."

"One more month, that's great, Marcus," Peter said.

"How much longer do you have to stay in Vietnam?" I asked Peter, when Carla and Marcus went dancing.

"Six months."

He became quiet and I was feeling uneasy because we were alone. But he sighed and sat back to look at the sky. "Back home," he said, "the Big Dipper's over there." He waved his hand vaguely in the air.

I tilted my head and located the Big Dipper, wondering how the constellations could move when one was in another place. A multitude of stars shimmered in the sky; the moon was a mere crescent. A soft breeze was redolent with jasmine, gardenias and dama de noches.

Peter took a deep breath and said very softly, "That

feels good." He paused then spoke in a distant voice. "It's real funny, but sometimes, in the middle of nowhere, I'll think of my baseball cards. When I was a kid, I collected baseball cards — Willie Mays, Mickey Mantle, Ted Williams — I had them all. But I don't remember what happened to them. My mind starts going through the entire house. I'll search my room, my sister's, my parents' room, even the garage. I rummage through all the desks, drawers, and cabinets. It's crazy. I've even written my Mom to ask about those cards."

He sighed, then he turned to me and said, "That's a real pretty dress."

"My friend doesn't like it very much."

I laughed remembering Turtle Face. He grinned and ran his hand through his hair. I had never before seen hair as red as the mangosteen fruit. My apprehension left me and I watched the stars with him. He liked the night and things of the night. These made him feel safe, he explained, in a way that implied he didn't feel safe too often. When we saw a falling star he gave a quick low whistle. "Now I can make a wish," he said.

As he was pointing out Orion's Belt, he put his arm around my shoulders, his fingers brushing my nape. My heart pounded against my ribs, but I didn't move or say anything. He was so close and I could smell him — a strange, musky scent. He was quiet for a while then with his other hand, he turned my head toward him and he kissed me. His mouth was warm and yearning. There was a sadness to his kiss. It made me think of Sultan and how warm he had felt before he became still.

When Carla and Marcus returned, Peter kept his arm around me, but the spell was broken, the magic moment lost.

The next day, I listened to the American planes blasting overhead. Was Peter in one of them? I wondered. Would I ever see him again? I looked at my blue-green chiffon dress lying on a chair — it was magical after all.

Another plane zoomed overhead, making the windows rattle, leaving my soul with strange reverberations. I thought: Summer vacation was over. School would start. The rains would come.

1521

THE WOMAN NAMED Old Healer had gone into a trance at the marketplace, and had predicted that their chieftain, Lapu-Lapu would have a son. This child, she said, would herald change for the islanders of Mactan. Thus on a March afternoon, the people sat outside the hut of Lapu-Lapu, anxiously awaiting the birth of his baby. Inside the hut there were only three people: Lapu-Lapu, his wife Buwan, and Old Healer.

For seemed an eternity, Buwan labored until at last the baby's head pushed its way out into the world, crying before the delivery was completed. The three cheered at the sound and Lapu-Lapu rose, telling the old woman, "Give me my son."

"A son?" retorted Old Healer. "And what if it is a girl? Shall we return it? Or shall we give it away to the Chinese traders?" Laying the baby face down on Buwan's stomach, Old Healer tied the umbilical cord, and shortly the birth was finished. After wrapping the infant in a colorfully woven blanket, the old woman handed his to the eager father.

Before uncovering the baby, Lapu-Lapu glanced at his wife and sheepishly said, "You know that I would love any child who is the fruit of our union, boy or girl alike." But later, he jubilantly held up the infant in the air, shouting, "You see, I knew from the lusty cry that we have a boy!"

Old Healer scurried around the small room and gave Buwan a sweet potato because she had not eaten in a long time. "Take your son out and clean him," muttered the woman. She was a Tausug from the south and could not comprehend the softness and sentimentality of the islanders.

Outside the villagers milled about, repeating, "It's a boy! It's a boy!" Someone said, "Hey, Lapu-Lapu, let's hope your son will be a better fisherman than you." People laughed, including the proud father who was on his way to the sea.

The islanders accompanied Lapu-Lapu and watched as he carefully submerged the infant in the water. The baby, red as a tomato but strong, made little swimming motions. The villagers cheered because the sea was an integral part of their lives, and they told the father that the child was truly a son of the sea like all of them.

Old Healer followed with the after-birth in a coconut shell and she instructed Lapu-Lapu to bury it. Handing the infant to Old Healer, he took the coconut shell and walked away from the people. With each step he took, the islanders called out his name and Lapu-Lapu resisted turning, for it was said that if he did, something bad would happen to the child.

After the ritual, the father sat on a boulder with the baby in his arms. He looked around him and it seemed as if the island of Mactan had never been more pleasing. There were coconuts, corn, tubers, and other vegetation in the fields. The tranquil water stretched out before him, shimmering and glinting like a million gems scattered under the sun. A tide pool in the coral reef teemed with fish, crabs, shrimps, and mussels. The good water surrounded the island and its gifts were plentiful. The spirits of the sea and universe were kind. All the spirits were good to Lapu-Lapu for granting him this boundless happiness at the birth of his son.

Shortly after the baby's birth, three big ships came from the east. The children, who had been swimming out at sea, stared as the vessels grew larger and larger, drawing near the larger island of Cebu across the deep channel. The children swam back to shore and scampered to the village with the news.

"Are these the trading ships?" the elders asked, referring to the ships from China, India, Vietnam, Borneo, and Siam.

"No, no, these are different," the children replied, "And the men wear metal clothes and they have metal weapons that shoot fire."

When Old Healer heard this, she recalled a dream when she was a girl about enormous ships with white men in them. She had forgotten the details of the dream but remembered its ill-flavor. "I have seen these ships and the men with skin like albino pigs," she said. "They will bring bloodshed and tears not only to us but to our grandchildren's children."

Concerned, the villagers sent Lapu-Lapu and the elders across the channel to meet with the leaders there. In Cebu, the men were divided. There were those who wanted to welcome the stranger. Raja Humabon, Cebu's chieftain, said, "These men have travelled far and are weary. We must help them. Perhaps we can trade with these people."

Lapu-Lapu, heading the group who wanted to get rid of the strangers, said, "The sooner they continue their journey, the better. A messenger from Limasawa island reported that these men shot their cannons at his village."

They argued back and forth but because the islanders from both places were peaceful people, they decided that Raja Humabon and his people would welcome them. As a precaution, many of their warriors would accompany Lapu-Lapu to Mactan in the event of trouble. In addition, most of the women and children would be moved inland.

The ships anchored; smaller boats were lowered into the sea and some strangers went ashore. One of them thrust a silver cross into the sand while those around him fell on their knees. They later sought out the leaders, offering them mirrors, bells, and trinkets. Through a Malay interpreter named

Enrique, the newcomers asked for water, fresh fruit, chickens, fish, and rice. They said they came from a distant place called Spain, and they had been at sea for two and a half years. Their emperor was Carlos, and their captain-general was a Portuguese, Ferdinand Magellan.

Among themselves the leaders repeated, "They will rest and go away." But two days after their arrival, the Spaniards installed a trading center at the market place and bartered mirrors, combs, wax, and other items for food and gold. A few days later, their monks preached of their God and baptized over eight hundred islanders, including Raja Humabon's wife whom the monks renamed Juana. Spanish expedition groups made drawings of the terrain and vegetation and scribbled notes about the habits of the islanders. The soldiers watched the movements of the islanders. They even captured some women, holding them captive on the ships.

Old Healer had moved into Lapu-Lapu's hut after her husband died, leaving her alone. She helped Buwan with the housework and because she knew the use of herbs and had the gift of healing, the people would see her when they were ill. "I have been bewitched, Old Healer, and my stomach hurts. Can you help me?" or "I have cut myself, please heal the wound." And most of the time she would cure them.

Buwan loved her like her own mother and one night, when from the corner of the room Old Healer moaned, "Do not go, stay. Not the water" -- Buwan hurried to her side. "What's the matter, Old Healer? Everything's all right."

Old Healer sat up and held Buwan's arm. "I had a dream," she said. "I dreamt that these white men cast fishing nets into our waters. They spat and pissed into the sea. Then they drew their nets. When they lifted them, I saw, not fish, but people — our people. These men took spears and pierced the squirming people one by one. Their brown skins burst and blood flowed down the nets into the sea.

"Go back to sleep, old woman. It's just a dream," Lapu-Lapu's voice boomed across the room.

Buwan tried to calm the woman. "Go to sleep. It is

nothing. Perhaps the pork you ate for supper did not agree with you."

The old woman tightened her grasp and pleaded, "Do not go into the water because they will cast their net. Promise me that you will stay ashore."

"You speak of nonsense, Old Healer," she said, but to pacify the woman, she finally agreed to avoid the sea.

The next day, when the sun's rays beat down relentlessly, Buwan forgot her promise. With her son in her arms, she wandered to the seashore where the women and children gathered. It was cool there and the water was pleasant. The mothers talked while the children played in the water. They did not notice the rowboat with three Spaniards who had been drinking fermented palm drink. The youngest one rose unsteadily and, aiming his musket, fired at the people. The women and children screamed and scattered. The Spaniard grabbed another musket, aimed and fired, hitting Buwan and the baby. The infant fell into the water that immediately turned red. With bloody arms, Buwan groped in the water until she found the little body that looked like a mangled piece of meat. Shouting, she shook him, as if trying to wake a sleeping child. The women had to pull them apart.

Old Healer later cleaned Buwan's arms. She tied them at certain points, put ointments on the wounds, and said Buwan would be all right. She then cleaned the dead infant and prepared his body for the burial that day.

The people came, chanting and calling out the baby's name during his burial. They placed a miniature boat, carved out of wood, on his grave. This would bring his spirit to better fishing waters. Before returning to their huts, they built a fire so the smoke would purify them.

Instead of going home, Lapu-Lapu went to the seaside. As he watched the water subside from the reefs, he remembered that not too long ago, he had sat on that boulder and had been filled with immeasurable joy over his son's birth. Now every muscle in his body was knotted in grief.

Raja Humabon remained hesitant about fighting the Spaniards, but the elders and warriors of Mactan clamored for war. "Let us burn their ships," one said. "Let us poison their food and water," another suggested.

Knowing about Lapu-Lapu's grief, they turned to him and waited for his words. "When we go fishing or hunting," Lapu-Lapu began, "we do not poison the water or our bait. We use our wits and we give the prey the chance to use his. This is the honorable way. We will fight these intruders. There are less than a hundred of them. We will destroy them like insects. But they must have the opportunity to use their wits."

All day they worked on a plan and when night came, two warriors burned the makeshift Spanish garrison in Cebu. Making sure the Spaniards saw them, they hurried across the channel. Early the next morning, sixty armed Spaniards, led by Ferdinand Magellan, went to Mactan in three boats. Not finding the villagers, they looted and burned the huts.

From their hiding places, one thousand five hundred warriors watched. Their blood boiled in fury as they waited for Lapu-Lapu's signal to strike. Lapu-Lapu watched the sea and, when the tide was low, ordered his men to attack. With arrows, javelins, stones, and spears, they fell on the surprised Spaniards who frantically ran to their boats only to find them resting at different angles. The water line shimmered half a mile away; the Spaniards were trapped.

Recognizing Magellan, the warriors threw spears, scimitars, and lances at him. His left leg was hit, then his right arm. He struggled on the reef but Lapu-Lapu finished him off.

A cloud of gray smoke lingered in the air when the battle was over. Lapu-Lapu kept Magellan's body as a memorial of their victory, but he allowed the islanders to load the other corpses into the boats which they towed back to Cebu. This was their way of honoring the dead Spaniards who had after all fought fiercely. This was also proof to the remaining strangers that although islanders were gentle, they knew how to fight.

The women wept for all who died. Pointing out the body of a young Spaniard, a mother said, "Why, look, this one still has milk on his lips." She cried for the mother across the water who would suffer over her son's death.

Four days later, the surviving Spaniards left. As the people watched the ships sailing away, they thanked the Creator. They brought food to the burial grounds to thank the spirits of the dead. They tried to resume their lives, but an uneasiness had rooted in their souls. They knew that if these men had found their way to their place, others would follow. And what would happen to them? How long could they resist cannons and muskets, when what they did best was living, not killing?

Twenty-one years later, a Spanish exploration party returned to Mactan and Cebu. Old Healer had long been dead. Lapu-Lapu and Buwan had three more sons. They with the other islanders fought the conquistadores, but they lost, and a Spanish settlement was established in Cebu.

ALBA

Malate, Philippines (July, 1763)

I SET THE BUNDLES of thread near me and I pick up the dead boy. He is seven, maybe older. It is difficult to tell. He is extremely thin and his head is too big of his body, making him look like a shriveled old man. His rags reek of urine and feces. The wounds on his legs had festered until the poison travelled throughout his body. There is a huge gash near his right eye.

Other street urchins cower behind the battered, moss-covered church walls. Before the English came, there were stalls laden with Chinese silks, European brocades, and Mexican tapestries against those walls. Under that sprawling acacia tree, a toothless man sold copper cuspidors and silver-framed mirrors.

I remove my cotton *panuelo* and clean the boy. I lay him down and pick up my thread. His corpse will be carted away and burned along with the other bodies that litter the Walled City of Manila and its surrounding villages.

As I walk toward the seashore, I curse the English and Spaniards. To think of it — you carry a child in your womb for nine months, you nurse him, watch him grow, only to have him killed before he is even a man. If the child's mother saw her son, she would feel the anger I have when I remember my

71

grandmother's corpse.

The sharp edges of the *nilad* grasses scratch my legs and arms as I go through the swampy shore. I recall my grandmother, Lola Juana, pounding herbs with her marble pestle, saying life is a silver cord connecting us to a maker. A gift, she said. Life must not be wasted.

Turning, I see the galleons and English ships tossing on the blue-green bay. The air is damp and the sparrows flutter excitedly, seeking refuge in the coconut trees. A storm is coming. I hurry to my hut next to huge rocks. The strength of this bamboo and nipa hut, Carpio once said, is its ability to bend. The strong typhoon winds will not destroy this home.

My chickens and pigs scurry from the bushes to greet me and I herd them under the hut. Before climbing the short ladder, I give them water and I light a lamp. The wind is blowing and I feel my hut swaying. Below, the animals grunt and run around. I picture the bay foaming and the ships thrashing like coconut husks.

After eating some fish and rice, I work at my loom, alternating the colorful thread I bought today from the sly pockmarked peddler. I look with pleasure at the intricate bird pattern which I have created with blue, green, and red thread. Lola Juana taught me this design. The magnificent bird, she explained, became jealous at the first man's beauty and thus tried to peck out his eyes. But the first woman grabbed the bird's long and beautiful tail, scaring him away. I will give the finished blanket to Carpio. When the planting season is over, he will return. I smile, thinking of his fine brown body on this blanket.

The rain falls and its heavy pounding drowns the animal sounds. I finish a row on my loom and consider unrolling my mat when a clapping sound startles me. A girl's shrill voice rises above the whistling wind: Alba, Alba.

I open the window and peer out. Cold rain hits my face; there is only blackness outside. Who's there? I call out. Epifania, she answers. Doña Saturnina sent me. I ask her in. The young girl's black hair is plastered wet on her skull making her look like a crow. She flaps her arms excitedly as she explains. Her mistress is in labor and has asked for me. There are problems, she adds.

I throw a blanket over my head, wondering why Doña Saturnina wants me and not some European-trained doctor. There are many of them in Manila. We hurry through the swamp and I remember Doña Saturnina's visit a year ago. It was before the English came; it was drizzling, unusual for September. I handed her a piece of cloth to dry herself with, but she did not stop shivering until she saw my plants, my baskets, and my weaving loom. She said, My servants speak of your special powers.

There are fantastic tales about me, I answered. Some say I can turn into a dog or bird, or that I eat unborn babies. A woman accused me of making all the coconuts on her grove fall by merely walking nearby. My grandmother was murdered because of those stories. I am a simple healer. I use herbs and things of nature to help people.

Her eyelids flickered and I knew she had indeed heard those stories. I hold her father responsible for Lola Juana's death. He called himself a Catholic Defender and accused many of being heretics and witches. He incited the people to such a state that one night, Lola Juana was hacked to death by the village drunk. A black dog with glowing eyes attacked him, he related, and he was only defending himself when he used the ax. He was acquitted.

Lola Juana was my only relative. My parents and two sisters died of the fever when I was an infant. My grandmother raised me and taught me everything she knew.

That rainy September, I eyed Doña Saturnina with contempt. She sat erect next to my loom, looking like a typical Manileña. She had clear brown skin and her silky black hair swirled up and was held in place by a finely carved ivory comb encrusted with pearls. The jewelry on her fingers flashed red and green. I felt a coldness as I stared at her. I wanted to say I could do nothing for her; I wanted her to leave, but Lola Juana often said that healing is a gift from the Maker and one so gifted must use it.

Doña Saturnina's voice was low and sad. Her somberness reminded me of the black Madonna of Antipolo. Her husband, Don Diego Torres, had a constant buzzing in his ear, she murmured. This began after his brother died of the pox.

Without seeing him, I could do nothing. I told her this, but she insisted that I must have something for him. Finally, I gave her herbs from the enchanted forest and explained how to make tea from the dry leaves. She handed me a gold coin. At the door, she hesitated. The truth is, she whispered, I am here because I am barren. Help me, she pleaded in that melancholy voice.

She had seen midwives and European-trained doctors. She had made numerous novenas and pilgrimages, but she remained childless. Once, she said softly, she had thought of throwing herself into the Pasig River, so her husband could marry a fertile woman. He wanted an heir. His brother's death made him the last of the Torres family. I had heard of the Torres haciendas and galleon investments. They were almost as rich as the Spanish friars, the people said.

Doña Saturnina's hips were slightly narrow, but she appeared to be in good health. Her breath was sweet and her eyes clear. I gave her powdered bones of the flying lizard and told her to take a pinch, mix it with water and drink it every day. I made no promises, but she was grateful.

Now, Epifania leads me to the carriage at the end of the muddy trail. The driver beats the horse as we splash through the roads of Malate. We pass the church where I saw the dead boy. In the darkness, I can make out the beggars huddled against the walls. We turn a few streets and enter the Torres estate. The enormous house looms in front of us, surprisingly undamaged by the war. The English, Epifania explains, used the house for their living quarters. There was plenty of food and we were untouched by the war, she adds with pride.

Shortly after Doña Saturnina's visit last year, there was

a freak storm. I was at the rectory giving the old Spanish friar ointment for his rheumatic legs. He was telling the story about the Madonna and Child when news came that thirteen English warships were at the bay. The English were demanding the Spanish authorities to surrender, but Archbishop Governor Rojo insisted on defending the Walled City. Rojo had six hundred poorly equipped soldiers; the Englishmen, Draper and Cornish, had five thousand men.

I watched the villagers pile their belongings into carts as they fled for the mountains. In just a day, the English captured the villages surrounding the Walled City. They used the solid stone structure of the churches for garrisons, and from there they bombarded Manila.

There was bloodshed everywhere — men, women, and children, maimed if not killed. Women were abused by the English. Houses burned down in a few minutes. Manila — the Pearl of the Orient — was destroyed in a few days.

Epifania guides me through the huge and elegant rooms with high ceilings. We walk past elaborately carved furniture. There are Persian rugs on the polished wooden floors and European damask draperies hang in front of capiz-shell windows. Don Diego Torres grasps my arm when he sees me. He is a wiry, graying man, much older than his wife. He has the furtive look of a forest creature. He leads me to the room, begging me to do everything I can to help his wife. She is all I have, he says. Help her; she asked for you.

The room has the sour smell of sweat and foul air. I instruct Epifania to open all the windows. A spray of water hits the windowsill and a crisp breeze fills the room. There are clean blankets on a chair and there is plenty of hot water. I wash my hands in the pink-flowered basin near the bed.

Doña Saturnina is curled up on her side. If not for her huge belly, she looks like a girl with her dark hair spilling around her. I put pillows behind her back and help her to a sitting position. She stares at me. Her brows are deeply furrowed. I feel her stomach to check the baby's position.

The bags of water broke this afternoon, she says. Labor

began this evening at sundown. The furrows between her eyebrows deepen as a contraction takes hold of her. Was your grandmother a midwife? she asks. I nod. She says nothing else.

The baby is a footling breech. A good-luck child — if it lives. I have never assisted in such a birth, but Lola Juana talked about such a delivery. Be very careful, she warned. Pull one foot, then the other, and the rest of the baby will slide down. If the mother is narrow, the baby may get stuck and both will die.

She tenses and winces. A contraction. Take a deep breath and let it out slowly, I tell her. I show her how and she follows me. Her body relaxes.

Later she says: I had nothing to do with your grandmother's death. I was only a child like you then. The memory of Lola Juana's mutilated corpse flashes in my mind. The men found pieces of her body in the plaza. Like a giant puzzle, they put her together. Swirling darkness swells inside me.

Once, she continues, I saw you. You were just a girl, walking to the river with a bundle of clothes on your head. You were with the other laundry women. I had my porcelain doll from Sevilla and I wanted to give it to you. But I could not.

Another contraction comes and she holds her breath and bears down. Not yet, I say. I look at her face and realize that she was indeed a mere child then.

She stares at me, her dark eyes flashing like that of a mad dog. Kill it, she hisses between her teeth. I feel her forehead, thinking she is delirious. If it's not dead, kill it, she repeats. Her skin is damp and cool. She cringes; there is another contraction.

So this is why she wanted me here, I think. I remember Lola Juana — she smelled of herbs; she was wise and warm — and darkness rises to my throat. I feel tired. If I do nothing, they will die. The tiredness fills my joints, the tips of my hair. She is drenched with sweat, her enormous stomach heaving with a life of its own. If I do nothing, they will die, my mind repeats. But Lola Juana's voice silences mine: Life is a gift; she is a woman in labor; and I am a healer.

The baby will be born feet first, I explain, as I reach for the infant's feet. I continue: When the head passes through the birth canal, the pain will be terrible. Then it will be over. Push with all your might when I tell you.

The baby slides down, then stops. Push, I instruct Doña Saturnina. She strains but the baby does not move. I tug at the little body and its head pops out. The infant is bluish in color and its mouth is wide open as it cries lustily. Doña Saturnina's eyes are closed as she breathes rapidly. It's alive then, she whispers.

I wait until the umbilical cord stops pulsating, then I tie the cord. I tell her to push one last time and the placenta comes out. I check this thoroughly, heeding Lola Juana's warning. A woman bled to death because a piece of the placenta was left in her womb.

I wipe the blood and cheesy covering from the baby boy. He is swiftly losing the bluish color and he appears strong and perfect. I hand him to her. The very fair skin of the child next to her brown skin startles me, and then I understand. She looked hesitantly at the infant. Her eyes become watery and tears spill down her cheeks. He's small, she says as she looks at me sadly as if seeking forgiveness. It's not his child, but he is mine, isn't he? she asks.

I help her hold the baby against her breast. The infant roots wildly until he finds her nipple and he sucks contentedly. This one will live, I think. An English bastard and a good-luck child.

I wash and comb her hair into a bun at her nape. If you wish, I will take the child, I tell her softly. She does not answer. She is stroking the baby's face and body.

I clean the bed and room before calling Don Diego Torres. He rushes to me, eyes wide with anxiety. She lives? he asks. I nod. His sharp features soften and he weeps. Holding his breath, he walks slowly toward the bed. Don't be afraid, I say, your wife has a boy. I close the door and wait, fearful for the infant, but all I hear are hushed cracked voices.

The carriage is waiting but I prefer to walk home. The rain has stopped. There is a soft dawn and a mild sea breeze. I breathe in the cool, tangy air as if to cleanse my spirit. I look back at the huge house and see a morning star shining faintly above. I am surprised that I feel no rancor. Some birds fly past me to their nests in the battered church walls. I think of Carpio. I must finish my blanket so it will be ready for him when he returns from the fields.

THE DISCOVERY

1

Mama's letter sounded just like her: "You father is getting worse. You have been away for three years; it is time for you to come home." Just like that. As if she were telling me to brush my teeth or else I would get cavities; as if she did not three years ago, in a fit of anger, accuse me of causing Papa's stroke when I married Robert, otherwise known as "the American" by my family.

The letter instructed me to pick up plane tickets for myself and my one-year-old son Dan from the travel agency. Perhaps as an afterthought, she wrote, "I hope that Robert comes over. The family wants to meet him. Your uncle liked him very much."

My mother's brother had visited us and had unsubtly cross-examined me: "How old is he? Twenty-nine ... very good. What does he do? Ah, a psychiatrist ... very good." Apparently he had returned to the Philippines with glowing reports about 'the American.'

The last paragraph was Mama's usual gossip section. "Your cousin Josie finally left that husband of hers. That lunatic was bringing his mistresses home. The latest gossip is Luis Mendoza's marriage to some girl — a complete unknown.

Floring is heartbroken about it. You know how she wanted Luis to marry well. Write me your flight information. Love, Mama."

It was so typical for Mama to be casual over such matters. Like telling me that Papa was worse, or like telling me to "come home" after three years of silence. Her two-sentence report of my cousin's desertion did not at all elaborate on what a scandal it no doubt was, and how the family's name was probably sullied as far as Manila society was concerned. And then there was her casual remark on Luis' marriage. In a few words she reminded me again that it was her wish as well as his parents' wish that we should have married. The wedding of the year; a big family wedded into another. A consolidation of land and power. To me Luis meant the first bitter-sweet experience of love. But that was a long time ago.

Still it was good to hear from Mama and even Bob was pleased that after three years my mother had 'forgiven us.'

"And why shouldn't she?" I asked. "After all, she eloped with Papa. One day she walked out of the house and ran off with a thirty-two-year old widower. My grandfather was violently mad. Mama was only eighteen.

It was a shocking thing to do back in the thirties when Philippine society clung to the conservative Filipino-Spanish ways. My grandfather, "Don Marciano," as he was known, refused my father's proposals of marriage to my mother, so one day, he rented a plane and brought my mother to another island where they were properly married.

Whenever the story was told, Mama would be the shy young girl all over again and she would say, "I didn't want to go. I was so scared. I kept saying 'no' but he insisted." Meanwhile, we children would act out the scene, only whoever played Mama's part would eagerly run toward the imaginary plane saying, "No, no, I'm scared."

Robert couldn't take the time off from work and said, "Well, as long as my rival is married. I guess you can go. Besides Dan will drive off any dirty old men."

2

The stewardess came up to me and said, "Can't you do something with your child? He is bothering everybody." She turned leaving me in tears with my squirming, screaming child. If only Bob were me with, I kept thinking, everything would be fine. Then I thought of taking the first flight in San Francisco back to Los Angeles and to just forget the whole thing. But somehow I survived the twenty-hour flight to Manila.

When I got off the plane, I was totally exhausted. I had rings under my eyes, my hair and clothes looked miserable, and my mother clucked her tongue and said, "*Madre mia*, you look terrible. We must take you to the beauty parlor right away."

At home Papa's room smelled of sickness and it pained me to see my emaciated father lying there as helpless as a baby. His eyes flickered when he saw me. He tried to speak but saliva dribbled out. I wiped it off and talked to him of my life in the States, what my husband did, what I and my son did. I told him that he had to get well so he could visit us. He cried and all I could do was hug his frail body and tell him that I loved him and that everything would be all right.

The next night, my brother and his wife held a *bienvenida* party for me. Practically everyone I knew attended.

"Cathy, you look ver-ry ver-ry pretty," an aunt said.

"Mama had me remodeled at the beauty parlor, Tita Merced," I replied. And she did. The same day Dan and I arrived, she had me turn Dan over to *yaya*, and she took me to the beauty parlor for a haircut, facial, manicure, and pedicure. Afterwards, she brought me to Makati to buy clothes for myself and Dan. She proudly pointed out the new buildings, saying, "See, just like America, ha?" Still in a daze, I noticed very little. The heat was stifling; the traffic and noise gave me a splitting headache. Everything seemed unreal — first I was in one country, then I was in another. But it felt good to be back.

"How do you survive without maids? I am getting *loca-*

loca, plain nuts, because one maid left," a cousin said.

"Well, I brought my own maid with us to Washington," another voice piped in. Why don't you order a servant from the province? Just don't get a pretty one or else she'll run off with an old-timer like Floring's maid."

I had forgotten that servants were "ordered" from the province and handled like pieces of furniture, and one suffered the occasional inconvenience of their leaving your household.

"That one was really bad," Floring, Luis' mother, spoke up. "I was glad to get rid of her because she was such a thief." Turning to me, she sighed and whispered, "You could have had everything you wanted, *hija*, if you had married Luis."

"But Floring, you know how young people are. They do as they please nowadays," my mother said, as I made my exit.

It was interesting to note that I was no longer the 'baby of the family.' I was now a young matron married to a successful psychiatrist, and even the snobbiest aunt treated me with deference. I found it embarrassing and wished they would treat me like an awkward ugly duckling as they used to do."

I looked at the people around me and I couldn't believe how much I had changed in three years. I couldn't believe that I had been like them just a few years ago. So westernized. Faces turned to the West: speaking English and Spanish, watching Hollywood movies every week, reading American magazines, dancing to rock and disco music. Faces turned away from the East toward the West, away from the people.

Something was wrong. In the United States, I had remembered the comfort of having servants and the beauty of fine things. My family and my friends still lived in this pretty world. But I was seeing things beyond this tinseled world. There was another universe present. There were poor and hungry people. Men and women queued up to get water from fire hydrants; one-room shacks made from boxes, newspapers, tin, and pieces of wood; beggars in tattered clothes with their empty tin cans. And the numerous dirty, half-naked children, rummaging through the trash for scraps of food. They were there; I had never seen them before.

"Mommy," I said on the way to my brother's house," the people are so poor."

Startled, Mama looked at the big-bellied children playing in the gutter. "Yes," she replied, "they are dirty. They should stay in the province and not in these slums."

"They have nothing wherever they go, Ma."

"They can farm; they can fish. *Por Dios*, why do you think God gave them intelligence, two hands, and two feet?"

"But farmers and fishermen are still poor, Ma. Why is that?"

She shifted her gaze from that other world and said, "I don't know, *hija*, God's will." And she casually shrugged off centuries of poverty suffered by my—by our—people.

3

I had difficulty sleeping after the party. When I finally did, I had vivid but disoriented dreams of a Filipina wearing a long black skirt and a mestiza top. Her face appeared drawn and haggard. I knew she came from a funeral and there was sadness and deep regret in her heart.

There were flashes of other scenes. I saw this woman as a young girl walking with a man. They were surrounded by flame trees dripping with clusters of scarlet flowers. The man reached out tentatively for her hand. She looked at him sideways and smiled.

In another scene, the man was telling the girl that he was leaving for Spain. He needed his freedom, he said. He would be gone for a while but would return to marry her. The girl wept.

The last vision was that of a wedding. The girl, resplendent in white, stood next to a European man. Although she smiled and laughed at her wedding party, she was unhappy.

I awoke feeling uneasy. There was something familiar about this dream. In a way I had done the same thing. Luis told me he wanted his freedom. When I heard he was actually seeing other girls, I left for the States. I, too, married a foreigner.

Luis found out about my marriage from my mother. According to her, he lost weight and he would visit Mama practically every day and just sit there, not saying a word. A year after my son was born, he got married.

4

In the morning, while eating pan de sal and drinking coffee, I told Mama about my dream. She decided that the poor woman's soul was in trouble and we should have masses said for her. As we chatted, the maid announced that we had visitors. Mama and I went to the living room. An older woman wearing a simple green shift and a younger woman in jeans and T-shirt stood waiting for us. My mother blanched when she saw them.

"What are you doing here? How dare you. Get out!" My mother's hand went up and struck the older woman's face.

"Señora, we just want to see him. Before he dies. He … has never seen our daughter," the older visitor said. Mama's arm swung out and I held it. "Get out!" Mama said. "You'd better leave," I said. They left. "How could she do this?" Mama said. She sat down, shoulders hunched, a defeated look in her face. "I gave her money to go far away, to have her child far away and never come back," she cried.

"Ma, was that girl Papa's —"

"Yes. That servant spent more time swaying her hips than taking care of you. And men, you know how they are. Weaklings. I told her to stay in Bulacan for the rest of her life. I gave her money. Why must she torment me now? What else does she want?"

She wept and I held her tenderly, stroking her graying hair, realizing how much she had aged during the time I was gone and during the time Papa was ill.

"You don't know what I've been through. The scandal, the shame. Double standard. Men have *queridas* while we stay home. Maybe divorce is better. So many wasted years. I have suffered much." I had her in my arms. I was the mother and she was my daughter. Her shoulders were shaking and I remembered how I had wept over Luis' deception years ago.

5

We had been in Manila exactly a week and I was still feeling tired from jet lag and the heat. The past days had been hectic and I was relieved to learn that Mama had a dinner to attend that night. I could have some time to myself.

I was reading in my room. Everyone in the household was asleep. The house felt empty. I remembered my dream and I shivered. I looked out the window and the long shadows cast by the trees brought back childhood fears of *encantados* and witches. I checked the spot where the nun had been buried. After the war, my parents had found the decomposed body of a Paulist nun stuffed in a barrel. They had buried her in our backyard. Servants spoke of seeing her ghost near the area.

The ringing of the doorbell startled me. I slipped on my slippers and ran down. The complicated locking system confused me and I fumbled with the chains and knobs for several seconds before I unlocked the door. I protectively drew my robe around me and peeped out. It was Luis -- and magically, it was five years ago.

"What are you doing here?" I opened the door and gestured for him to enter.

"I can't stay long," he said.

And I couldn't help myself. "Yes, your wife's waiting. Sit down." I sat across him.

"You look the same, as beautiful as ever," he mumbled and I laughed and pointed at my robe to show how unglamorous I was. "You look the same, Luis," I said. He did. The same longish face with glasses. The same voice. I wanted to cry but managed to carry on a light conversation about our visit. The baby had insect bites and he was sleeping and would he like to see him?

"I came to see you." His voice was very sad and we kept quiet. I looked at him and around us. It was unreal; the moment had the quality of sunset-like a crack between two realities. Neither night nor day, neither past nor present.

"Your hair's still long. Hey, I'll bet Americans like long black hair." We laughed and the bond was still there. "Do you remember," he said, "that day, the first time we really met?"

I nodded, recalling that May day when the childhood friends had met, not as children, but as a young man and a young woman.

"I was just sixteen. A spoiled brat. I'm much better now," I said jokingly, hoping he would laugh.

He would not stop. "It was raining the first time I held your hand. Do you remember?" And on and on he reminisced in that pained voice. And I kept thinking, your wife is waiting for you, because it seemed to keep the tears from falling.

And then I said it: "Your wife is waiting for you, Luis."

The words sounded cruel. He got up and I led him to the door. He paused. "You know I still love you," he said, and walked out.

I stood there scarcely breathing, listening to his fading foot, steps. The seconds were slowly passing by when something compelled me to run after him.

"Wait, wait a minute," I said, oblivious to what was or wasn't acceptable. "I have to tell you something important because I don't know when or if I'll ever see you again. I still love you."

He began caressing and kissing me. "I love you," he said. "Leave him and come with me. I would leave my wife to be with you. I love you very much." He would not let me speak. "We don't have to live here. I can work in London. We can live there," he continued.

"Luis, I'm so confused. Let me think things over. I don't know what I'm doing right now," I replied.

"See me tomorrow. I'll meet you tomorrow afternoon at the Zamboanga Cafe. One o'clock. Will you be there?"

I nodded.

6

The next day, I told Mama that I would spend the afternoon with my college friend, Araceli. What I planned was to go to Bulacan in the morning and meet Luis at the cafe in the afternoon. I wasn't sure why I wanted to see the maid and her — my father's daughter. Curiosity, perhaps? Or perhaps I wanted to meet my half-sister.

I drove to Bulacan and had no trouble finding their place. Their house was better-looking than I expected. There were children outside who asked me whom I wanted to see, and they ran screaming into the house announcing my presence.

'Señorita, please sit down," the older woman said as I walked in. "This is such a surprise. Linda, bring Coke for Señorita."

Her daughter soon returned with soft drinks. I looked at her. She must have been a couple of years younger than myself. She looked a lot like my brother. A small boy — around three years old — hung on to her skirt. Something about the child made me stare at him. The older woman noticed and with a hint of pride said, "This is Linda's child. The father is a very important man in Manila ... the son of Don Fernando Mendoza.".

I choked on my drink and I glanced quickly at the boy. Yes, he did look like Luis. My mind was racing. He wasn't married to Linda because he married someone else recently, which meant Linda was his mistress, or former mistress.

The pit of my stomach tightened and I got up and said, "I just came to meet you. I'm sorry about what happened at home." I felt a chill inside me. "I have to go now. Good-bye." I rushed out of there and drove for hours around the countryside, watching the farmers bob up and down as they pushed rice seedlings into the watery paddies. I did not meet Luis at the restaurant that afternoon. Without any explanations, I told the people at home that I did not want to talk to Luis if he should call. Every time the phone rang I felt faint.

7

To amuse us, Mama took us to Fort Santiago. "You'll like the dancing waters," she told Dan. The Fort seemed smaller than the image in my memory. Perhaps it was because this memory had been imprinted in my mind when I was a little girl. Or perhaps it was because I had seen larger and grander castles in other parts of the world. Before Dan was born, Bob and I had travelled around Europe and I had been particularly enamored with the Alhambra in Spain. The Fort Santiago was a small corner of the Alhambra. It seemed curious to me that the Alhambra had been built by the Moors but that the Spaniards eventually expelled them and took over the magnificent fortification. Fort Santiago had been built by the Spaniards and the Filipinos in turn got rid of the Spanish conquistadores and took over this Fort.

The three of us wandered around. I noted the Fort's massive walls and its strategic location—right at the mouth of the Pasig River which must have been the lifeline of the ancient Filipinos. We looked at the fountain with rainbow lights shining on the rippling water. The garden within the Fort had tropical flowers blooming in riotous colors. We walked toward Rizal's shrine. We entered the museum and looked idly at Rizal's things: his clothes, the sketches he drew, pictures of his Irish wife Josephine Bracken. We visited the room which had been his prison cell. A picture caught my eye. It was a photograph of Rizal's first love, Leonor Rivera. She was up on a balcony and her long black hair hung loosely around her. She looked young, and although she was not smiling, I knew she was happy.

As I stared at the picture, a memory of that moment started forming in me. It was as if I could see the Pasig River which lay in front of her and the yard by the side of the house. The feeling of deja vu swept over me and recognition came that this was the girl in my dream.

"I wonder if she was happy married to that Englishman?" my mother said.

"Who? Leonor Rivera?"

"Yes, if she loved Rizal, why did she marry someone else?"

"She loved Rizal very much, more than he loved her. But there were some things she could not accept and she married another man." I turned away from the picture. "She should have told him that she still loved him despite everything. Leonor was always sorry that she never told him."

My mother looked at me quizzically but was quiet.

8

It was difficult saying good-bye to Papa because I knew I would never see him alive again. The nurse had just bathed and changed him. His hair was plastered down like that of an infant's. His body was wasted and he seemed to hang on by a thin thread.

"Pa, we're leaving at noon." His eyes widened and welled with tears. "I'm sorry Robert could not be here. You would have liked him, Pa. He is a good man. A decent man, very even-tempered and calm. And he loves me a lot, Pa. He is very good to me."

The silence was deafening. The pain in my chest was more than I could bear as I kept my tears from falling. I wanted him to remember me happy.

"Pa, I never told you this before, but thank you for everything. You gave me everything I needed. You sent me to the best schools. You were always good to me." It started to rain and there was a soft pitter-patter on the roof. He shut his eyes and tears slipped down his cheeks to the pillow.

"Do you remember that pink dog? I still have it, Pa. You bought me that toy when we went to Escolta one time. I wanted it badly but it was very expensive so I didn't ask for it.

But you saw me touching it and you got it for me. Thank you, Pa. I love you very much. Good-bye."

I kissed him and went to find Dan so he could kiss his grandfather good-bye. Then we left.

It was still drizzling when we arrived at the airport and my mother was getting sentimental. I sensed his presence" before I saw him. Before he got to where we were, I went to him.

"I'm sorry, Luis."

"I waited for you the whole afternoon, the whole afternoon. You even refused "to talk to me over the phone. My mother told me you were leaving today."

"Luis, I know about your child in Bulacan. Linda is my halfsister."

"What difference does that make? I love you. What difference does Linda or my wife make? We love each other."

"Luis, I care for you. But I have to go. I have another life somewhere and it is a good life. I have to give it a chance. Take care of yourself and let me say good-bye now, before I cry and make a fool of myself."

In the plane, a young nurse immigrating to the States sat next to me. She didn't see Dan who had obligingly gone to sleep.

"Is this your first trip to America?" she asked. "No, no, actually, I'm going home." I looked out at the bay and the city with many memories for me.

ABOUT THE AUTHOR

Cecilia Manguerra Brainard is the author and editor of over twenty books including her novels, *The Newspaper Widow*, *Magdalena*, and, *When the Rainbow Goddess Wept*. She has also co-authored a novel entitled, *Angelica's Daughters, a Dugtungan Novel*. Among the books she edited are *Growing Up Filipino: Stories for Young Adults* and the follow up book *Growing Up Filipino II*.

Her work has been translated into Finnish and Turkish; and many of her stories and articles have been widely anthologized.

Cecilia has received a California Arts Council Fellowship in Fiction, a Brody Arts Fund Award, a Special Recognition Award for her work dealing with Asian American youths, as well as a Certificate of Recognition from the California State Senate, 21st District. She has also been awarded by the Filipino and Filipino American communities she has served. In 1998, she received the Outstanding Individual Award from her birth city, Cebu, Philippines. She has received several travel grants in the Philippines, from the USIS (United States Information Service). In 2001, she received a Filipinas Magazine Award for Arts. Her books have won the Gourmand Award and the Gintong Aklat Award.

She has lectured and performed in worldwide literary arts organizations and universities, including UCLA, USC, University of Connecticut, University of the Philippines, PEN, Beyond Baroque, Shakespeare & Company in Paris, and many others. She teaches creative writing at the Writers Program at UCLA-Extension.

She is married to Lauren R. Brainard, a former Peace Corp Volunteer to Leyte, Philippines; they have three sons.

She has a website at ceciliabrainard.com and a blog at cbrainard.blogspot.com.

Published books by PALH (Philippine American Literary House)

Benedicta Takes Wing and Other Stories by Veronica Montes

Growing Up Filipino: Stories for Young Adults edited by Cecilia Manguerra Brainard

Growing Up Filipino II: More Stories for Young Adults edited by Cecilia Manguerra Brainard

Please, San Antonio! & Melisande in Paris (novellas) by Eve La Salle Caram and Cecilia Manguerra Brainard

A River, One-Woman Deep: Stories by Linda Ty-Casper

Kindle Titles by PALH (Philippine American Literary House)

Fiction

Acapulco at Sunset and Other Stories by Cecilia Manguerra Brainard

Awaiting Trespass (novel) by Linda Ty-Casper

Benedicta Takes Wing and Other Stories by Veronica Montes

Contemporary Fiction by Filipinos in America edited by Cecilia Manguerra Brainard

The Black Man in the Forest: Short Story by Cecilia Manguerra Brainard

Fiction by Filipinos in America edited by Cecilia Manguerra Brainard

Flip Gothic: Short Story by Cecilia Manguerra Brainard

Growing Up Filipino: Stories for Young Adults edited by Cecilia Manguerra Brainard

Growing Up Filipino II: More Stories for Young Adults edited by Cecilia Manguerra Brainard

Magdalena (novel) by Cecilia Manguerra Brainard

The Newspaper Widow (novel) by Cecilia Manguerra Brainard

Of Midgets & Beautiful Cousins: Short Story by Veronica Montes

Out of Cebu: Essays and Personal Prose by Cecilia Manguerra Brainard

Please, San Antonio! & Melisande in Paris (novellas) by Eve La Salle Caram and Cecilia Manguerra Brainard

A River, One-Woman Deep: Stories by Linda Ty-Casper

A Small Party in a Garden (novel) by Linda Ty-Casper

Vigan and Other Stories by Cecilia Manguerra Brainard

When the Rainbow Goddess Wept (novel) by Cecilia Manguerra Brainard

Wings of Stone (novel) by Linda Ty-Casper

Winning Hearts and Minds (1967): Short Story by Cecilia Manguerra Brainard

Woman with Horns and Other Stories by Cecilia Manguerra Brainard

Nonfiction

Cecilia's Diary: 1962-1969 by Cecilia Manguerra Brainard

Fundamentals of Creative Writing by Cecilia Manguerra Brainard

Magnificat: Mama Mary's Pilgrim Sites edited by Cecilia Manguerra Brainard

www.ingramcontent.com/pod-product-compliance
Lightning Source LLC
Chambersburg PA
CBHW050310260626
47156CB00005B/1743